Tunnel Vision

Tunnel Vision

Ronald Phillips

Printed in the U.S.A.

Published by
Ronald Phillips
109 Limekiln Drive
Neenah, WI 54956

Printed by
PrintSource Plus, Inc.
1314 W. College Avenue
Appleton, WI 54914

Printed in the United States of America

ISBN: 978-1-4675-7663-5

Library of Congress Control Number: 2013909883

Prologue

It was May, 1997 when Mike Dennis, Ike Tenner, and John Nelson graduated from the prestigious Colorado School of Mines in Golden, Colorado. All three were receiving their Masters Degree.

Over the past three years in school, they formed a very close bond of friendship. They felt more like brothers to each other, rather than classmates. When Ike lost his father in an auto accident two years ago, they all felt the loss. Each celebrated their victories and supported one another when deep sorrow was evident, as was the case with Ike's father.

They were intelligent, they were confident, and most of all they had an adventurous spirit. Their eagerness to venture out would allow them to take chances and embrace life and challenges that they would likely encounter.

Upon graduating from college, they had a plan which was conceived during the last six months of studies prior to graduation. Their now three year friendship was solid and steadfast, and they believed it would serve as a basis for sometime in the future forming a business partnership.

They were acutely aware that they were inexperienced and had much to learn about mining and general business practices. School was a theoretical approach, treating mining as more of an exact science than what would be faced in a real world environment.

Each of the three students had two summer

internships that introduced some level of actual mining practice into their foundation of realistic mining activities. They were astute enough to grasp how little they really knew.

The three men had carefully investigated different companies to be contacted for first jobs. They had earlier agreed that working for the same company would not be in their best interest. They chose dissimilar types of mining corporations so they could collectively draw on a larger array of experience when they eventually formed their future partnership.

As the years passed since their graduation, they stayed in touch with each other as much as possible. That commitment to remain connected took extraordinary effort on each of their parts. Their respective employers were headquartered in different western states. That factor was compounded with extensive travel requirements for Ike Tenner and John Nelson. In most years they would try to coincide their vacation schedules and that aided the continued cementing of their relationships.

As time went by, Mike would marry and start a family. The other two men remained single. Staying single was more the result of long hours and extensive travel obligations than actually ever wanting to be alone in life.

Mike was the "thinker" of the trio. He was very much into mine administrative management where as the other two were more operational and "hands on." Mike moved up quickly in his company. Ike and John gained minor promotions and were moving forward in their careers at an average pace.

Mike was the impetus for conceiving their eventual partnership program. Mike had vigorously studied the history of abandoned mines and it was his theory that some very old mines might not actually be "played-out." He felt that some mines, if properly re-worked utilizing modern technology, could potentially yield a profitable payoff.

Mike spent several years researching old mines which ceased to be operational. There were thousands of such mines throughout the southwest. Some of these abandoned mines were originally incorporated and later went bankrupt. Some mines were just abandoned and the operating company that worked the mine simply went elsewhere, leaving a hole in the ground. As research goes, some records on a mine's history were very good. However, for the most part, quality information on terminated mining operations was scant and hard to obtain. None-the-less, Mike was a relentless student of research, even to the point of contacting older miners (if they were still alive) to get information that was not in any written archives.

In 2004, Mike stumbled on the Dodd/Hickey Mine abandoned in 1917. This was a great silver producing mine from 1906-1915. The original owners reaped riches at the time. Then as usually was the case, the ore vein ran out and further mining was quite uneconomical. This abandoned mine and surrounding land changed hands four times until it was finally surrendered to the state out of the interest of public safety and lack of ownership connection to any remaining organization. The Dodd/Hickey Mine and surrounding land had been in state control for almost thirty-two years.

Mike had determined that the characteristics of the played-out silver vein in the Dodd/Hickey Mine were quite different than what he saw happening in most mines that were abandoned. He formed an opinion that with today's advanced modern mining technology, this mine could be reopened. He was quite confident that there was a better than fifty percent chance that this mine could still produce silver ore.

Mike, of course, contacted Ike and John. It didn't take much persuasion to get both of them aboard Mike's plan. Both Ike and John had been frugal and they anteed-up fifty thousand dollars each into the new partnership. Mike did the same, however, in Mike's case half was borrowed on his home as a second mortgage.

The mine was bought with all mineral rights for a mere $20,000. It was a steal if a silver vein still existed. If not, their partnership venture would be a short-lived affair. It was a very big gamble for everyone. Mike worked the plan and took care of the acquisition. Ike and John agreed that it was best if they kept their jobs until the mine "proved-out" and could actually yield profitable operations.

Mike had contacts and through them he obtained a $100,000 loan at a fairly high interest rate. With the $130,000 still left from their starting capital and the $100,000 loan, Mike opened the mine.

Mike left his job in September, 2004. The mine opened that same fall with Mike at the helm and a crew of six miners under a six months work contract.

Mike saw few results from the mine for the first

sixty days. His disappointment in himself was growing. Worse, he felt badly for Ike and John who he convinced to invest their savings.

On day sixty-one, the foreman of his contract team came into his trailer office and dropped a nine pound rock on Mike's steel gray desk. Mike jumped back from his chair from the loud crash as the rock thudded onto the desk. Quickly, Mike looked up at the foreman who was grinning and then peered carefully at the rock. The silver vein in the rock was pronounced. For Mike, it was a thrill beyond compare. If this rock was any indication of the silver vein which was being discovered, his ownership in the Dodd/Hickey Mine would be worth a fortune.

Fast forward six months and the partnership had all three members as full time employed partners. Ike and John had quit their old jobs in December 2004. The mine now had thirty-six full time employees and was operating two shifts daily. Millions of dollars of silver ore were being pulled from the mine with no indication that the vein of silver would run out.

The Dodd/Hickey Mine success repeated itself two more times between 2005 and 2007. Four mines were purchased from the state. Two were mistakes, but the other two provided rich veins of copper.

By the end of 2007, the partnership was worth over one hundred million dollars. A partnership headquarters building was planned in Golden, Colorado very close to their alma mater. The new building was finished in late 2008. It was a timely piece of construction, as space was badly needed by the firm which now was running six very profitable mines.

A stranger driving through Golden, just might look up and see a beautiful stone and glass headquarters building. Featured in glistening black slate letters at the top of the fifth floor was Dennis Tenner Nelson Mines Ltd. The building was exquisite and it clearly accentuated the careers and fortunes of the three owners which were being propelled forward at light-speed.

Chapter 1
April 8, 2009

Mike Dennis sat at his Chairman's desk with intent interest, flipping through reports covering last week's ore production, financial statements, and a few resumes. At times, the drill of review and sign-off approvals became tedious, and Mike would look out of his fifth floor corner office window at the surrounding suburbs of Golden, Colorado. At times like these, he would envy Ike and John who could get out of the office into the field and first-hand be involved with exploration and mining activities. Occasionally, he would venture out also, but his programmed inspection visits were too ceremonious and orchestrated.

Mike stood at the window day-dreaming when his intercom interrupted the silence, as Mike's secretary announced Paul Fisher was here for his 10:30 a.m. appointment. Mike replied to send Paul in right away.

Within seconds one of the carved double wood paneled office doors swung open. Paul Fisher briskly walked into the office and stood at the front of Mike's desk. Mike quickly took in Paul Fisher's overly thin frame for his six foot two inch height. Paul was quickly motioned to become seated, as Mike took his seat behind his desk.

At the same time Fisher was seated, he placed a cup of coffee on the front of Mike's desk on a plastic coaster he brought with him. Mike, not one to stand on ceremony, was not upset by the bold coffee cup placement incident, and merely reached over his desk to shake Paul's hand and utter a cordial "good morning, Paul."

Paul Fisher like most of the professionals on the staff had a mining engineering degree. Mike looked to Paul more than others on his staff because Paul was a terrific researcher. In fact, Paul was mentored by Mike Dennis to sleuth through abandoned mine records looking for the proverbial needle in the haystack. Once each month, a meeting would be set up in Mike Dennis's office where Paul Fisher would go over any possible discoveries from ongoing research activities.

Mike with a gracious wide smile started off the meeting. "Well, Paul, have you come up with anything since last month? You know we need to keep one step ahead of the creditors and keep the doors open for another week or two." This was Mike's jest of friendly sarcasm, knowing full well that the firm was extremely wealthy and was currently enjoying an outstanding business year.

Paul Fisher was not one to catch the nuances of Mike's humor and just started into his business presentation with only the slightest smirk at Mike's attempt to lighten things up.

"Mike," said Paul, "I have three possibilities for you to look over. I am not sure you'll like two of them but the third one is intriguing. The Norman III Mine in Boulder closed in 1951. Records are scarce here. The best I could make out was that the copper vein started to get too thin and the owners just walked away. It is not in state hands and I can't seem to get a good picture of where ownership lies. It has gone through two estates and now every owner seems to be a decedent. This will take a lot of legal work to get solid ownership and you have to decide if that is worth doing."

"Okay, let's put that aside for now. What's next?" Mike was very focused because discovering old mines had made the firm very rich. Mike felt he had the "midas touch" for making good decisions on what abandoned mines would work out for the firm.

"The next one," Paul went on, "is the Brandan Ford Mine in Alamosa, Colorado. It was foreclosed in 2007 because the owners declared personal bankruptcy. It still had operations going for lead mining when everything came to an abrupt halt."

"Too fresh on abandonment plus I don't want to get into lead. Just too little yield for my taste." At that point, Mike rose from his chair and went over to a small refrigerator at the corner of his office. He grabbed a bottled water and asked Paul if he also would like some water. Paul declined.

Paul continued as soon as Mike reseated himself behind his desk. "I saved what I feel is the best for last. I tried something new. I hired three university students to research archives for failed mining companies in Colorado, Idaho, New Mexico and Arizona. I set the parameters for research to mines which were in play for five years or more. Additionally, they had to be mines that were separated from any other mines by at least ten miles. I was looking for isolated abandoned mines that would be pretty well forgotten. This approach yielded less than I hoped except for the Timberlake Stake Mine in Alamogordo, New Mexico."

Paul hesitated for a moment and then pulled

several sheets of paper away from a file folder he had carried into the office with his coffee cup. With a more serious tone, Paul spoke as he handed two sheets of paper across the desk to Mike. "The Timberlake Stake Mine lies by an old dried out lake bed. This mine was a low producing gold mine that was just barely profitable enough to keep the doors open for about six years. It was abandoned in 1912. The land and the mine are controlled by the state of New Mexico. I like the characteristics of this mine because it was deep. It was recorded to be down to almost 800 meters when it was left abandoned. We have the technology now to go much deeper. Further, from the research I received, they only hit a top vein of ore." As Paul went on, he reached across the table to point out items to be read by Mike on the sheets of paper previously pushed in Mike's direction.

Paul started again with a more enthusiastic tone of voice. "I really believe there is a secondary vein still lower. We have seen this scenario before in other mines. To me this looks like a replay of the famous Dillon Mine in California, which was re-opened ten years ago with a solid gold vein below what was thought to be a small higher elevation gold vein."

Mike sat back in his chair with a contemplative look and studied the report provided. As he held the report in his hands, he spoke with a strong level of authority. "You know Paul, you just might be right about this being a worthwhile enterprise if we dig deeper. There are a few things I would like you to do now to follow-up on the Timberlake Stake property. Personally, go down to New Mexico and quietly follow up on environmental concerns. Visit the mine area and look around. Do not enter the mine. Check out local old records to see what you might learn. If there are relatives of descendants of some of the original miners, make a discreet call or two. Also, find out what local law firm has any expertise in dealing with mining issues. If we go forward, we need a local presence." Mike reeled off about a dozen more suggestions as Paul furiously made notes.

After the meeting, Mike called both Ike and John to tell them about the Timberlake Stake Mine. Both were enthusiastic. Both Ike and John felt Mike had an uncanny knack for securing good profitable properties. They saw no reason not to pursue the lead.

Chapter 2
May 6, 2009

Two weeks earlier Paul Fisher had returned from his investigative trip to Alamagordo, New Mexico. He had been there for almost an entire week researching archives, speaking with key individuals along with personally visiting the mine area several times.

Paul's report was delivered to Mike a few days ago. By this time, Mike had read the report three times. Several calls were made to Paul when Mike had additional questions about the mine. Now Mike stared down at the one half inch bound report as it sat on his desk. Mike rose from his chair and looked out his window at a gray rainy day. Off to the west there was a hint of clearing in the sky.

After a few minutes of day dreaming out his window, Mike began to focus. He had made his decision about the Timberlake Stake Mine. Mike quickly picked up his telephone and dialed the number of Frank McCarthy who was the firm's corporate attorney at Billings, McCarthy and Travis.

The call was put through to Frank McCarthy who picked up on the second ring. Mike Dennis announced himself and there was a few minutes of cordialities and small talk. Fairly soon Mike began to discuss the purpose for his telephone call. "Frank, we just finished researching a new property that we want to go forward with as a mining project as soon as possible. The property is called the Timberlake

Stake Mine and is located just outside of Alamagordo, New Mexico. I am going to copy my research reports and have them delivered to you this afternoon. Frank, somehow, my gut intuition says this might be a really good property. However, I want to proceed cautiously on this one. I would like you to set up a separate New Mexico corporation where our firm will own an eighty percent interest. I will find the other twenty percent ownership from key locals in Alamagordo. We need the locals to have a stake in this to grease the support we require through the various levels of local and state government."

Frank McCarthy listened carefully, taking notes along with asking a few questions during their conversation. At the end of hearing Mike Dennis's request list, Frank began to comment. "Mike, this is definitely a can do list of items. However, to get all this done and to buy the mine is going to be a six months timeline at best. How much capital are you planning to use to initially fund this new corporation?"

Mike was quick to reply, "We'll fund the new company for about three million dollars. We will have to take it very slow at first. I would like to target getting into the mine by November." The telephone call continued for ten more minutes eventually moving toward discussing personal matters and a two o'clock tee time on Saturday.

After the call, Mike set up an afternoon meeting with the Chief Financial Officer of the company, so cash needs for the new venture could be planned in advance.

Mike then proceeded to call Ike Tenner and ask

if he would have any objection to taking charge of the Timberlake Stake operations. He carefully covered the planning particulars. After hearing what needed to get done, Ike was enthusiastic about spearheading the project.

The next six months sped by. Every step for opening the Timberlake Stake Mine fell neatly into place. The start-up costs turned out to be less than Mike had figured, leaving most of the three million dollars of capital infusion investment still in place to fund actual mining operations.

During this six months interval until the Timberlake Stake Mine began operations, general business for Dennis, Tenner, and Nelson Mines Ltd. was robust. All existing mines were strongly producing quality ore at good market prices. The net worth of the company was growing exponentially.

Chapter 3
December 1, 2009 - January 28, 2010

Mining operations had started for the Timberlake Stake Mine. The first few days were exclusively spent evaluating the mine for safety issues. Painstakingly, steps were taken to perform the necessary actions to correct for any safety concerns noted. The abandoned mine was already 800 meters deep when operations started. Safety was of critical importance, thus beginning activities went very slowly to make sure the structural integrity of the mine was sound. At this significant depth into the earth, extra precautions were taken to make sure "rock bursts" could be avoided.

After three weeks, the mine was down to 835 meters with no sign of any ore vein. It was quite disappointing, but management was prepared to go to 1,000 meters before considering the venture a lost cause.

On January 28, 2010 Mike Dennis picked up his ringing phone just as he was entering his office for a new day at work. It was 7:45 a.m. as Mike glanced at his watch. He was a little startled to get a call this early in the day. Mike answered, with announcing his name, "Mike Dennis here." That was the start of the telephone conversation as he put the phone to his ear.

"Hi Mike, this is Ike Tenner. I hope I didn't catch you too early in the day. Us working guys start early you know!" The friendly sarcasm was stated with a short chuckle at the end.

"Hi Ike" responded Mike. "It's always nice to hear from the underworked field personnel."

"Yeah, right," retorted Ike.

"So what's up buddy?" Mike questioned.

"Well, here it goes Mike." Ike was serious now and down to business. "Yesterday we hit the 890 meter depth level and broke a drill bit. Then we broke two more drill bits and stopped work. We cleared away some rock and found we hit something I have never encountered before. So far, we cleared away about a sixteen square foot area where we broke all the bits. There seems to be a hard black surface showing up that seems quite impenetrable. We tried going around the problem, but this hard surface seems to be quite extensive. Before we do anything else, I think you better get down here as soon as you can."

"Ike, I'll arrange for a charter plane if it is available on short notice. If successful, I should be there in the afternoon sometime. In the meantime, try to clear away as much rock as you can from this hard surface. Maybe with still more rock cleared away we can get a better view of what we are dealing with." Mike finished the call with a short good-bye. He next called his wife and told her an emergency came up at the New Mexico mine and not to expect him home that evening.

Mike was always prepared for these quick emergency trips. He kept a packed suitcase in his office. He quickly called the airport and arranged for the charter to Alamagordo. Mike also arranged for a rental car and a hotel for the night. Another charter flight was set up for the next day's return to Denver. Mike was at the mine by 2:45 p.m.

Chapter 4
January 28, 2010

As Mike Dennis was driving up to the mine site, Ike was topside waiting to greet him. Ike handed Mike some coveralls so he would be properly dressed to descend into the mine. The elevator ride down the mine shaft took about six minutes. It seemed a very long ride down to Mike. By the time they reached the 890 meter depth, Mike was impressed at how deep this mine was dug.

Where the miners were currently digging, was a cleared out area of the mine shaft of about 600 square feet. When they arrived at the area, three other miners were clearing away rock from the unknown object they encountered. The black object remained an impenetrable surface. Rough rock had been cleared to expose about sixty square feet of surface area.

When the men arrived from the mine shaft elevator, all work ceased so that Mike and Ike could get a first-hand look at the black slab of object that had been uncovered. Mike approached cautiously, and then put his hand directly on the black surface. It was very smooth to the touch and a little cool temperature-wise. To Mike, it felt like obsidian, but he knew that it was not obsidian. Mike then grabbed a rock pick and hit at the surface fairly hard. He was surprised by the sound of impact. He expected a sharp report, but the actual sound he heard was very subdued, much like the sound of a hammer hitting soft soil. He repeated hitting the surface a few more times with the same result of hearing a very soft thud. It was a remarkably strange sound for everyone present to witness.

As Mike and Ike continued to gaze at the exposed surface of the black object, it appeared that this surface area did not seem to be of any natural origin. The smooth cool feel seemed to have a manufactured look which seemed very puzzling.

Mike looked over at Ike who was running his hand over the smooth black surface. When Ike looked up, Mike said, "Let's go up. I think we need to talk." At that point, the two of them walked back to the elevator. On their way, Ike turned to the three miners present and requested they try to clear away more rock from the black slab.

Once at the top, they sat together on the back of a tailgate of a parked pick-up truck. Topside the temperature was about 53° with a light wind. The sky was clear. It felt refreshing to be outside, after being in the elevator mine shaft. Mike looked over at Ike and started their conversation. "Whatever that object is, it is not a natural phenomenon. I don't have any clue as to what it is, but clearly someone put it there. I have a very strong feeling we need to keep this "find" very secret until we know a whole lot more. What do you think?"

"Mike," Ike quickly retorted, "I am on the same page as you are. Clearly when we dug to the 890 meter level, we had to excavate virgin rock. There was absolutely no evidence of an object being put in the ground and covered over. Our dig was a fresh excavation through fairly dense rock. What do you think our next step should be? Also, by the way, at our current 890 mark, there is still no sign of a deeper gold vein."

"Listen Ike," Mike went on, "Let us for now close the mine. Reassign all the workers to other projects. Tell anyone in Alamogordo, who we have a connection with, that we are giving up on further operations and immediately closing the mine. We need a period of silence here so the Timberlake Stake project seems abandoned. When you wrap things up here and get back to the office, let's meet. In the meantime, I'll bring John up to speed as soon as I return. Other than John, everyone else is to be informed we are closing down operations.

Ike gave an affirming nod and walked with Mike back to his parked rental car. As Mike drove off, Ike went back to the mine.

As it was dusk, Mike drove to his hotel in Alamogordo and set up his return charter flight to Denver in the morning. At the hotel, Mike worked out a tentative plan concerning the next moves for the Timberlake Stake project.

Chapter 5
February 9, 2010

A little less than two weeks had passed since the order was given to close the mine. All workers had now been reassigned. Interested parties in Alamogordo were disappointed to hear of the mine closing, but they took the news in stride. Locals were used to failed mining projects. The Timberlake State Mine property was now closed up and vacant of all personnel.

On February 9, 2010 a meeting was held at 1:30 p.m. in the Executive Conference Room at Headquarters. The meeting was attended by the three principal partners of the firm.

Mike started out the meeting. "In front of each of you is a typed plan about how I think we should proceed. Why don't each of you take a few minutes to look it over. By the way, I swore my secretary Nina to absolute secrecy, since I needed this in typed form."

Several minutes passed as both Ike and John carefully reviewed the plan in front of them. Each made pencil notes in various places. As they both finished reading, each looked up with an expression of showing they were finished reading the proposed Timberlake Stake step by step plan.

Mike began. "I checked with accounting and we have about $2,450,000 left to spend out of our original capital set aside for this project. My question to you Ike, since you have the most experience with the black object, what would it take to fully uncover a two hundred foot length of this thing, assuming it is that long or longer?"

"Well Mike," answered Ike. "This would be a rough guess. I think we need at least three months and maybe sixty truckloads of rock being extracted. Remember, I have no idea how long this object is, what shape it is, and how deep I have to go to get under it. I think we need to greatly expand our work area down there so we can set up heavier extraction equipment. I will need a two shift crew of twenty men on each crew. Keeping this activity quiet will be a challenge."

"I think this will be a very expensive process," Mike ventured forth a comment. "In fact the numbers for labor alone get pretty large. Forty plus miners at a premium pay for three months, plus equipment and other attendant costs is a major enterprise. I figure that it will run about $3,500,000. Are you two guys willing to throw that kind of money into the pot to see what we found?" Mike looked up after his question so as to give the impression he was looking for some reaction.

John was first to comment. "You two have seen this thing first-hand. I'll go with the flow here. If you vote to go ahead, then I'm in it with you."

Quickly, Ike spoke up with his comments. "How can we not go ahead! For my money we just can't let this go. If the firm can afford it, I say we need to see what we have discovered."

"Well, then, let's go for it." Mike had a very excited tone in his voice. "Ike, are you still okay with staying down in Alamogordo and continuing to oversee this project?"

"Hey, Mike, I wouldn't have it any other way."
As Ike took a sip of coffee, he looked up and went on.
His voice was very enthusiastic. "I can do this project
on a stealth basis so that we keep locals in Alamogordo
in the dark. I know back roads we can use to shuttle
equipment into the area. We need tarps to cover the
mining activity, so aerial flights in the area will not be
alerted to our restarting the mine."

"Ike, you and John need to create a listing of
our forty miners. I would suggest guys you can really
trust. It would be advantageous to use men who are
single, without family responsibilities, if at all possible.
These guys are going to be on site for the better part of
three months. That's a really long time to be away from
home. This has to be a premium pay deal to keep these
guys happy and also silent about the project." Mike
continued. "When you have made your choices as to
miners selected, get the group together so I can provide
them with some specific instructions, before you bus
them down to New Mexico to get started."

There was some continued back and forth
conversation as the meeting drew to a close. Mike went
over once more, the step by step action plan he had
created before the meeting. The meeting ended at 3:30
p.m.

Chapter 6
February 22, 2010

Mike looked out his window and took note of a stream of cars coming into the company parking lot. These would be the vehicles driven by the miners who were told to report to headquarters for an early morning meeting.

It was 8:30 a.m. in the morning, as the carefully chosen forty miners were assembled in the company auditorium. In addition to the miners, were Mike, John, and Ike at a head table. Also invited were the CFO of the company and Mike's secretary. When all were seated, Mike stood up and walked over to the podium. The room immediately became silent.

"Good Morning," Mike began. The attending group of miners felt compelled to answer back with a responding, "good morning."

"A few months ago, we opened the Timberlake Stake Mine near Alamogordo, New Mexico. Our plan was to go deeper into the mine and hopefully, hit a secondary gold vein. The original gold vein played out when the mine was abandoned in 1912. The mine was already down to 890 meters when everything stopped. Our new operation was headed up by Ike Tenner and a small staff of miners. In fact, two of those miners are among you today."

"To go on, after a few weeks of drilling and excavation, we hit a solid object that we could not identify. It was clear to us that this object was man made. What is so incredible is that it was struck at the 890 meter level. So far this object is impenetrable and our drill bits just break apart on contact."

Mike reached for some nearby bottled water, took a sip and then continued.

"We believe there is something important to be discovered here. Further excavation and uncovering more of this object is our primary mission. Any additional unearthing of this object must be handled with a high level of secrecy. With that said, all of you have been chosen as our most trusted crew. You must not mention anything about the Timberlake Stake Mine to anyone. To anyone you speak with, just say that you have been assigned to a New Mexico gold mine for the next ninety days, nothing more."

"I know ninety days is a very long time to be away. We are going to pay double time wages per hour. Also, if we eventually make any money from our discovery, ten percent of all profits will be divided up amongst this group of forty miners, who are assembled here today. Now please put your hands up if you are still interested in working on this project.

Forty miners threw their right hands up in the air. At that point, there was a lot of conversations among the attendees, until Mike was able to get the meeting back to order.

At this point in the meeting, Ike Tenner got up from his head table position. "I will be heading up this project and will be at the mine site with you for the next three months. I will now go among you and give you each a handout that I have created. This will give you details about what to bring with you and what you can expect for living conditions. Our group leaves on two buses that depart from our parking lot with a date selected by me. Please remember, confidentiality is of critical importance."

Chapter 7
March 1, 2010

Before the miners arrived on site, Mike had arranged for the quick construction of a pre-fabricated wooden housing unit. It was a quickly improvised two hundred foot building that housed bunk beds, four bathrooms, and a makeshift dining room and kitchen area. Additional, port-a-potties were provided for outside the mine and still more to be lowered to the work area at 890 meters. Substantial food and supplies were stockpiled. Four powerful generators and necessary diesel fuel were also set up on site.

The miners arrived on site in the late afternoon of March 1, 2010. After arrival, it took two days to re-open the mine, do necessary safety checks, and set up all equipment. Work began in earnest on Wednesday, March 3, 2010. When the miners finally got a chance to view the black slab object, they just shook their heads in bewilderment. Generally speaking, the entire crew was anxious to get started.

The daily work was tedious at best. Considerable time was spent greatly enlarging the mine work area at the 890 meter level. This was important so there would be adequate room to erect scaffolding around the object. The noise level was incredible, and Ike had to get sound-proof helmets for the miners to wear in the work area where excavation was occurring. Cutting away rock from the object and removing debris from the mine shaft was difficult work, and the process was slow.

Ike made twice weekly progress reports to Mike, as more and more of the object was exposed. After thirty days, two hundred feet of length was uncovered on the top of the object. The more difficult task lay ahead. The next job would be to clear rock from the sides of the object, and eventually beneath the object, if at all possible.

By April 30th, 2010, the project was completed and miners were released except for a skeleton crew. Mike and John were yet to visit the mine. At this point, the cost to get the 200 feet of the object fully uncovered was $4,500,000 . . . a $1,500,000 overspend from the original $3,000,000 set aside in the beginning for the Timberlake Stake project.

Ike made a final call to Mike, for both he and John to visit the mine and view the final result. Ike would not elaborate on the phone as to what was eventually discovered. He said John and Mike had to see the uncovered object for themselves.

Ike arranged for Mike and John to fly to the mine site in a charted helicopter on May 3,2010. This would be the moment Ike was working for, to finally show his partners what the true nature of the object looked like. Ike knew both Mike and John were in for a shock.

Chapter 8
May 3, 2010

It was a partly sunny day with a pleasant temperature in the mid-seventies when the chartered helicopter flew in to the mine site. A whirl of dust spread in all directions as the helicopter landed about two hundred yards from the opening of the Timberlake Stake Mine.

Both Mike and John were astonished to see the number of buildings erected. Beside the main two hundred foot building, there were four other smaller buildings used to store topside equipment in order to protect them from the elements and visually hide the equipment when not in use. Several three-sided shacks were erected to house each generator.

Two buildings of medium size were placed at the entrance to the mine. One housed a larger generator that was used to control the elevator and lift out cut away debris. Still another building housed an air compressor system with four large flexible ducts that snaked out of this building and went vertically into the mine shaft. Not far away, Mike spotted two large tanker trucks. One held fuel for the generators and the other said "water."

Every piece of equipment, the tanker trucks, and the buildings were spray painted beige to blend in with the color of the surrounding landscape.

Mike and John were quickly greeted by Ike as he approached their helicopter when the whirling blades finally stopped moving. "You're just in time. Welcome to our mystery spot. I'll bet you didn't see much evidence of our project here until you were right on top of it. Everything is painted sand beige to match the rock formations around here. We even sprayed our growing slag pile of debris pulled from mine."

At that point in the conversation both Mike and John looked to the right of the mine shaft opening. They saw a twelve foot high by two hundred foot long piling of mining rock extracted. They were both quite surprised at how much material was removed from the mine.

Ike continued. "Let's head down. By the way, we keep a crew of eight in place now. Two are always at the dig level and the other six are top-side to keep things running smoothly."

Mike and John put on coveralls before they ventured over to the mine opening. All three entered the mine elevator together. The quiet hum of the generator and the air compressor units were now evident as they began their decent downward. Mike immediately noticed the vertical shaft was twice the size compared to the last time he saw it. Also, a new larger elevator had been installed and put into service.

The descent to the 890 meter level now took about four minutes. It was a quiet ride and no one really spoke as they went deeper and deeper. As the elevator slowed, Ike said, "We're almost there. You guys are going to flip when you see what things look like."

All three men stepped off the elevator as it finally settled at the bottom of the mine shaft. Ike stepped out first and hit a switch by a wall of the cave. The cavern area went from low light to bright light in a matter of five seconds as spotlights sequentially initiated and brightened the area.

Mike and John stood there in awe as they viewed the entire excavation project first-hand. They saw scaffolding everywhere around the object. The object and surrounding cavern stretched out to almost the size of a football field. They judged the cavern area to now be about eighty feet wide and over fifty feet in height from low to high. As they walked in further they finally grasped what Ike had uncovered.

Before them lay a huge black pipe. It was absolutely massive. Ike explained that the uncovered pipe was oval in shape. Ike had measured the pipe and found the dimensions to be an unbelievable forty-eight feet wide and thirty feet high. Everywhere, it was all the same pitch black color that Mike had looked at months before. This pipe stood before them with a shining black surface reflecting the glow of lights from the overhead spotlights.

John was first to comment. "My God it's a pipe! But the size! I have never seen anything so massive. It's almost the size of vehicle tunnels that are built to go under rivers carrying traffic. Who or what could have the technology to put something like this so deep into the earth. I can only wonder what purpose it serves. Ike, have you been able to find any opening, so we can see inside this thing?"

Ike just shook his head. "There is no opening. Nothing at all. This is a surface like I have never seen or ever heard of for hardness. It is absolutely impenetrable. Our drill bits just break off on contact. We tried a small diamond tipped saw blade in one area, but it just shattered. We even blow-torched areas to see if intense heat would soften it. Not only would it not soften, but wait until you see this."

Ike went over to a metal box and grabbed an acetylene torch. He lit it up until a thin narrow blue flame shot out about four inches. For two minutes he attacked the surface of the pipe heating an area of about six square inches. Both Mike and John could see an almost imperceptible orange glow to the object where the torch was being applied. Ike then shut off the torch and asked Mike to touch the heated area.

Mike was quick to reply. "No way. I'm not touching that area."

Ike calmly went over and put his hand directly on the heated area with only twenty seconds since the torch was turned off. "This area is as cool as the rest of the pipe," said Ike.

Mike and John both followed suit and touched the heated area. It was cool to the touch.

John was shocked. "I've never heard of anything that could cool off that quickly. This material is beyond incredible."

Ike started again. "We poured several different types of acid on the pipe with no results. We even arranged for fifty gallons of liquid nitrogen to be applied to a small section of the pipe. We hoped we could super freeze an area and then chip away a frozen fragment. There was no effect what-so-ever. To sum it up guys, I have tried everything I could think of to break into this object or chip a section off. Nothing has any effect at all."

Mike and John walked around the pipe, went

under it, and climbed the erected scaffolding to view all angles. They walked the full two hundred feet of length and marveled at the size. Everyone thought the same thing. How could anything like this get placed so deep into the earth.

Ike now made mention of a new fact. "I have a very interesting observation for you guys to consider. At first glance, the pipe looks like it is on a completely horizontal plane. In actual fact it is not. For the two hundred feet we uncovered, the pipe rises twenty inches at a perfect uniformed slant. It essentially rises from west going to east. Therefore, the reverse, of course, is that as the pipe goes westerly, it descends."

Ike continued, "The pipe is absolutely uniform in its dimensions. No variation at all. Every part of the pipe uncovered is forty eight feet wide and exactly thirty feet tall. This is precision on a scale that I have never seen before."

John entered into the conversation at this juncture. He was the mathematician of the group. "Let's presume there is a genuine purpose to this pipe, because the expense to put this thing into the ground is incalculable in today's cost. So let's assume the rise to the east stays uniform at one inch per ten feet. Let's further assume that somewhere there was a grand plan for it to reach the surface. If we assume it does reach the surface, we can extrapolate mathematically where it might emerge. I can run a mathematical model and hypotheticate the breakthrough point. I will need some time and a detailed terrain map of New Mexico, so I can account for rises in elevation. I know there are a lot of assumptions here, but I think it's a logical next step."

Mike was quick to follow up. "There is little more we can do here. Let's close this operation down for now. We can leave some things in place in case we come back for some reason. However, let's get our equipment to another mine where we have current operations."

At 4:30 p.m. all three principal partners of the company had returned to the surface. They said good-bye to Ike who would remain for a few days longer to shut down operations.

Chapter 9
May 19, 2010

At about 9:00 a.m. Mike sauntered over to John's office just down the hallway in the executive suite. Mike made two quick knocks on the doorway of John's partially closed door. As Mike entered, John looked up from his desk. He looked at Mike who seated himself across from John. "Mike, I guess you're here because you read over my e-mail this morning."

"You bet I read it. I am eager to talk to you. In your e-mail, you told Ike and I that you think you have it figured out where the pipe would emerge at the surface." Mike sat back smiling with a look of anticipation on his face.

"Yeah," John replied. "I ran a lot of computer models. Also I looked at several topographical maps of the potential emergence point in order to have a handle on rises and depressions in the terrain. You know Mike, there are a lot of assumptions here. For one, we assume the rise in the pipe stays fixed at one inch per ten feet of length. Secondly, we assume that the pipe continues on a straight course and does not curve for almost seventy-five to eighty miles of distance. All these assumptions are important to take into consideration, because I need to cover my tracks here. Any next steps on our part will cost the company a lot more money to go searching for the start point of the pipeline. Just so you know, I just checked and to date we have sunk $4,698,000 dollars into this project. Thankfully, we are having a stellar year, so we can afford a costly mis-adventure if that is how this turns out."

Mike sat getting a little impatient. "Okay, nice preamble. John you will be forgiven, if your guess doesn't work out. So what do you come up with using all your mathematical wizardry?"

"Mike," John blurted out with a certain tone of excitement in his voice. "My best guess is that our target area is about eight and one half miles east of Hagerman, New Mexico."

"Never heard of it," answered Mike with a somewhat cynical tenor in his voice.

"I've been checking Hagerman out very carefully. The town has about a twelve hundred population. Our target area appears to be a rather barren area with almost no vegetation. There are not any significant rock formations to contend with in the immediate area. I ordered a fly-by with a cameraman so I have photos of the area, if you are interested. The fly-by team has no idea why they were hired. They just took the job for the eight hundred dollars we paid them. I ordered a detailed plat map of the area under consideration for possible exploration. My research shows ownership of this property to be with a small local real estate company in town. This company owns a fair amount of land on all sides of Hagerman. I have not contacted this company yet." At this point, John finished talking and unravelled a three foot by two foot plat map with a large red circle around an area east of Hagerman.

Mike sat back digesting John's summary. After a few contemplative seconds, he responded. "In for a penny, in for a pound. I don't want to let this mystery go. Here are some suggestions. Please contact this real estate company and properly identify us. Give them some crap about satellite computer imagery and our belief that there could be several types of mineral deposits on their land east of Hagerman. It is best if you call as an owner of our company to squelch any suspicions that will certainly arise. See if you can arrange to give them $20,000 for a one year lease, and the right to drill test borings. The lease should give us a twenty year renewal option at $50,000 per year for full mining operations. Also, explain to them that as lessor, they will get a standard four percent of all extracted mineral revenue sold by us." John was making quick notes as Mike spoke.

Mike went on with further suggestions. "In addition, tell them that if we end up walking away, we will restore the land to its current condition. Get our law firm to draw up a contract before you speak with them. Make an appointment with the owner of the real estate company and personally go and see him to deliver the contract. No doubt after your meetings, they will check us out. Give them a few weeks to have their local law guy bless the contract. If all goes well, we should have smooth sailing to proceed by June. By the way, are you okay with Ike heading up the dig site and looking for an opening point for the pipeline entrance?"

"Give it to Ike please. I have a new wife, and like you, the dig site is too big a commitment for a married guy to be gone so long. Besides, I already talked to Ike, and he is as eager as ever to honcho the next phase." Mike rose from his chair and told John thanks for the update, as he headed towards the door.

Just as Mike walked out through the entranceway to John's office, he turned and quickly said, "I just have a hunch that you will find the pipe start point. If we do find it, our company is going to have some major decisions to make. Anyway, keep me posted."

Chapter 10
June 22, 2010

Mike picked up the telephone, as the call was forwarded through from his secretary. "Yeah, John, what's up?

"Mike the deal is sealed. I have the signed lease on an eight square mile tract of land east of Hagerman. When I first mentioned possible mining after test drilling, they thought we were crazy. In fact, the owners exact words were . . . 'If you want to throw away $20,000, fine, we'll be glad to take it.' Anyway, they did send the lease to a local attorney in town for review. Their attorney called me and said it would require a six percent royalty on extracted minerals versus the four percent we offered. I made it sound like a problem and called him back the next day with our agreement for six percent. I made it look like we caved-in on that point, and he had won a major concession from us. In my mind, six percent times zero revenue is the same as four percent times zero revenue. I'll bet for that tremendous concession, he told his client what he accomplished and probably will now bill him a thousand to fifteen hundred dollars for an hour of his time. Hey, this brings to mind a couple of lawyer jokes I remember. Anyway, the deal is done. I will get a $20,000 check off this week. Ike should be able to start the next phase of our project next week."

"John, you did a great job. Please get Ike up to speed on this matter. On a new subject, when you get a moment can you drop in to chat. I would like to discuss a couple of unrelated projects that might just happen in Utah."

Chapter 11
July 19, 2010

Many test bore drillings were set up by Ike. Three days of drilling had produced no contact with the pipeline. Ike had figured the best center point to begin and then he worked outward in concentric circles. Each drill down was to a depth of fifty feet, which everyone felt would be deep enough if their calculations on the rise of the pipeline elevation proved out. Knowing they had a forty-eight foot wide pipe to contend with, Ike set up a grid so each drill hole was made systematically so that there was not any way to miss the pipe, if it were there.

Drilling continued day after day. Every two days, Ike called Mike and provided an update report on progress. By the end of two weeks, Ike was pretty bored with the Hagerman search project. His interest in the project was beginning to wane. His crew of ten were also getting tired of the whole thing. This crew of ten were selected from the recent Timberlake Stake Mine operation so that a tight reign of secrecy could be maintained on the venture. Within two weeks eighty-eight drill holes had been dug.

On the eighteenth day in the field (July 19th) one of the drill crew ran over to Ike who was seated at a wooden plank table studying the plat map. The man was very excited, because they had just struck a very hard surface at a depth of ten feet. Ike came immediately over to the discovery hole. He mapped out five more test holes to determine the positioning of the pipe, if that was what had been just discovered.

In the next two days, eleven more concentrated test holes were dug. Then a quick dig down of a trench was made to confirm the existence of the pipe. Ike called Mike who directed him to do what was needed in order to find where the pipe started.

Chapter 12
August 1, 2010

Activities to find the pipe start point and clear out an opening area were in full swing. The actual pipe start point was located about four hundred feet east of the concentrated test borings which first hit the pipe. The opening was at a seven foot depth.

During the excavation process, Ike found it curious that the area in front of the pipe start point consisted of crumbled rocks as opposed to solid compacted earth. It almost seemed more like a hasty concealment was attempted at a later point in time.

A hole sixty feet wide and forty feet deep was created at the place where the pipe start point was found. The actual pipe start point revealed a vertical solid black flat surface that was true to the original pipe measurements. The vertical oval was forty-eight feet wide and thirty feet tall. It was exactly the same as the dimensions from the Timberlake Stake Mine. It was incredible to marvel at the craftsmanship.

Like the rest of the pipe, the vertical side with the flat beginning was impenetrable, showing no sign of any opening.

Mike was at the Hagerman site the day following the final uncovering of the pipe start point. "Ike, there has to be a door of some type. See if you can get a high resolution microscope that can be set up on a scaffold, so we can go over every square inch of this vertical surface area."

Ike responded, "Sure I can do that. It will just take some time to find what we need. Meanwhile, I am sending all the men home except for a crew of three, who will guard this area and keep any curiosity seekers away. We boarded up the area so no one can see anything from the road. We also have installed a large camouflage net that gets pulled over the dig site, so there is no aerial surveillance either."

Mike went back to Denver. Ike stayed to make some arrangements. His calls lent to renting a very high powered microscope borrowed from a university about three hundred miles away. It was trucked to the site. Since it was summer, the university relinquished the equipment at a high daily rental rate of $2,000 per day plus an insurance policy that was paid by the mining company, should there be any damage to the microscope.

It was absolutely incredible to view the vertical shiny black surface of the pipe entrance area at an enlargement of fifteen thousand times. What showed up about eleven inches in from the rim of the oval, was a crack. This crack was symmetrical at eleven inches going around the circumference of the pipe. A potential door opening had been found. The hairline crack was painted white so that everyone knew where the crack was in relationship to the vertical flat surface. If this were a doorway, it meant the inside dimensions of the pipe were forty-six feet two inches wide and twenty-eight feet two inches high.

Mike and John were called. Now that a potential doorway had been discovered, the problem now was how to get it opened.

Chapter 13
August 31, 2010

Continuous meetings of the principals of the company took place during August. Many suggestions were offered as each person tried to research and solve a way to open up the pipe through the presumed doorway.

On August 31, 2010, John Nelson came up with what the group felt was the best course of action. The company would rent four very powerful generators and adapt them with steel rods that had at least a four foot diameter suction cup at one end. The four rods with their suction cups would be placed at various strategic points in the doorway. Once the generator was activated, it would be designed to pull back on the steel rods away from the door. If the suction cups held firm to the smooth doorway, it might allow for a tremendous outward force to be applied. That force, it was hoped, might just exert enough pulling force to swing the doorway outwards away from the pipe.

It took three weeks to get all the right machinery in place. Everything was set up by September 23rd.

Chapter 14
September 23, 2010

The plan was not to initiate the equipment until Ike, Mike, and John could personally witness the first attempt to open the doorway to the pipe. By this point, the Timberlake project, as it was referred to, had cost almost six million dollars since the beginning, almost seventeen months earlier.

At 1:30 p.m. the helicopter landed and Mike Dennis stepped out with his briefcase in hand. Both Ike and John were already at the site waiting for his arrival before getting started.

Ike commented. "Mike, we are ready to get started if you are. We set up this first try with the four steel rod and suction devices on the left side of the doorway. We figured most doors open from left to right. If you guys are ready, I'll give the signal to start up the generators. The suction cups are already in place and seem to be tight to the door." Ike threw up his left hand in a circular motion which was the signal for a crewman to begin throwing a series of switches. There was an almost deafening groan as all four generators powering the screw-rod retractors kicked in simultaneously. The generators initialized and began to exert force towards pulling the doorway away from the pipe.

Mike had set his briefcase down to lean against the left side of the pipe just inches away from the white line marking the presumed door opening. He stepped back about ten feet and watched the process of the laboring equipment beginning to exert force trying to pull back the steel rods.

Everyone watched as the equipment strained to get the rods and suction cups to cause some movement outward on the doorway. Seconds ticked by as worry took hold that the suction cups wouldn't hold or the generators would overheat and fail.

Each second seemed infinitely longer in time as the equipment hummed louder and louder with the strain. It was so loud that it was difficult to talk above the noise. Ike shouted that the equipment was at half power, even though it seemed to Mike and John that a bursting point had already been reached. At the half power point, the rods were not retracting. There was not any sign of the door giving up its grip on staying shut. At three quarters power everyone noticed the door began to move a millimeter of distance.

The excitement was very obvious by everyone present. After a few more seconds there was a full centimeter of outward movement.

With a slight one centimeter opening, Mike looked down and saw his unlocked briefcase popped open and papers flying out. All the papers were being pulled toward the crack in the door opening. They stuck to the surface where the white line was painted. Dirt around the immediate area was being stirred up from the ground and was being plastered up against the white line. Quickly the briefcase itself left the ground and was now held fast to the slight opening at about four feet off the ground.

Mike became immediately frantic when he saw what was occurring. He shouted and waved but no one seemed to hear him. He ran over to Ike and grabbed his arm to get his attention. When Ike saw the fearful expression on Mike's face, he also saw Mike make a sign, like cutting his throat, and pointed to the equipment operator.

A quick second later, Ike got the message and immediately signaled that the equipment should be shut down. The machine crew responded, and quickly threw switches in reverse. It took about three more seconds before all the machinery was shut down. In that few seconds, the door which had reached almost two centimeters away from the pipe, reversed and silently slammed shut. The door was once again sealed tight to the pipe.

Once the doorway was shut, the papers and briefcase that had been held fast to the white line identifying the doorway opening, fell back to the ground. Dirt caked around the white line also succumbed to gravity and fell back to ground level.

Ike came over to Mike when all was quiet. "Mike, what gives? Why did you want us to shut everything down?"

With a nervous high tone to his voice, Mike was quick to answer. "This damn tunnel or pipe is a complete vacuum inside. As soon as there was a slightest crack of an opening, the suction forced my briefcase open. Didn't you see all those papers in the briefcase sticking to the doorway? Also, my briefcase itself came off the ground and was stuck fast to the door opening. If we had continued and had gotten the door open even to a few more inches, the vacuum pressure pulling outside air inward would have likely sucked us all in and we would have been killed. Can you even imagine the amount of air that would get sucked in if that door had completely opened?" Mike paused to catch his breath.

Both Ike and John stood looking at the doorway with their jaws dropped and their mouths open. "Oh my God, we could all have been sucked in and killed in another few seconds, if the door opened any wider. I never dreamed that this pipe would be a vacuum!" Ike went on. "How do we get around this problem? I think the equipment will get the job done at full power, and we should be capable of getting the door open. How we do it safely is another matter."

"Right," John chimed in. "We really have to be careful. I have an idea. I think we could build an iron chamber around the area near the door opening. Let's only allow air into the chamber from the top. If we can keep air from coming in from the sides, I think we can provide some level of safety, as the outside air whooshes in to fill the vacuum void."

Ike retorted. "That isn't a bad idea. I think we can rig something up so that we just pull in air from the sky."

Mike was quick to add his thoughts. "Guys think about this. We know the pipe is at least seventy-five miles long. We already have the width and height measurements. The amount of air going in will be phenomenal. I personally believe the suction will be so strong that air will be drawn in from a height of five hundred to a thousand feet. If birds were to fly overhead, they would likely get sucked in. We really have to give respect for the power of the suction force, that we would create when we get the door fully opened."

Mike continued. "If we pull air from the top, maybe we can set up a measuring mechanism to determine how much air rushes into the pipe. At some point, the pipe will fill up with air and the suction process will stop. If we had a handle on the volume of air intake, we could possibly calculate the full size of the pipe if the pipe dimensions stay constant. Our air intake calculations could lead to understanding how far this pipe is entrenched into the earth."

Ike lit up. "Give me some time, and I think I can set everything up. Then we can proceed safely and get a measurement on air intake"

Mike looked at Ike. "This is the most intriguing phenomenon I have ever seen. I don't know about you guys, but I don't think I can rest until I know what this pipe or tunnel is all about."

Both John and Ike nodded their heads in an affirmative motion. Everyone was very excited to do what needed to get accomplished to get the doorway completely opened.

Chapter 15
October 20, 2010

It was a clear sunny day of about sixty-five degrees when everyone congregated around the steel chamber that was erected to surround the pipe opening when the door would be pulled open by the generators and steel rods. A huge forty foot tall funnel was created above the iron chamber, so air would be channeled into the pipe from the sky. The funnel had been specially designed so air flow through the funnel could be accurately measured.

It was a tense moment when Ike gave the hand signal to start the generator initializing the screw rods to withdraw. As the roaring groan of the equipment hit three-fourths power, the door was giving up its hold on having been perfectly sealed shut. No one present could personally see the door being pulled open because the entire operation was housed in the huge iron chamber where there were not any viewing ports.

The noise of the equipment hit a peak of ear splitting decibels, as full power was attained. Immediately, everyone present was aware that the pipe door had been drawn completely open as they heard the deafening roar of air being sucked into the pipe at an alarming speed.

The suction of outside air continued unabated for thirty-six hours straight. The roaring noise was deafening and the entire crew stayed at least one hundred yards from the pipe, due to the loud unnerving sound of rushing air. A few of the crew had witnessed a hurricane. They remarked that the sound of air rushing into the pipe was very much louder. No one ventured close to the pipe, because the sound was so overwhelming. Finally, the noise stopped, which was a clear signal that the vacuum of the pipe was now completely air-filled. Soon after the noise stopped, a door to the iron surround chamber was opened. With flashlights in hand, Ike and John walked into the opening of the pipe. It was eerie, as they went into the pipe chamber almost one hundred feet. The blackness was unnerving and having flashlights gave small comfort as they lit up little around them. As the flashlights played along the inside surface, they could see the same shiny black smoothness that was evident on the exterior of the pipe. As they looked into the pipe with their flashlights pointed forward, they had the feeling that the open blackness was a gateway to infinity.

Mike helicoptered down the following day. The iron surround chamber had been pulled away and the now open pipe stood in front of them as a potentially dangerous and certainly ominous mystery to be solved.

Mike stood directly in front of the pipe entrance with a simultaneous feeling of amazement and bewilderment at the same moment. He said nothing as he was in a deep trance trying to imagine why the pipe was there, and of course also trying to understand its purpose for being.

Ike approached Mike. "Pretty scary isn't it? It is like we uncovered a doorway to hell, and maybe, we started something the whole world will live to regret. I am starting to have bad dreams just envisioning what is at the other end of this thing."

Ike went on. "We have measurements on the air intake flow. I would say our calculations are probably about ninety percent accurate. Since we know the chamber inside dimensions, we calculated the distance of the tunnel or pipe with regard to the vacuum chamber displaced with outside air. Believe it or not, if the chamber inside dimensions remain static, we came up with about twenty seven hundred miles long."

All Mike could say was, "No way in hell."

Ike kept on talking. "I know it sounds impossible, but that is what it works out to be with the air volume. Remember, when we first discovered the pipe, we were at 890 meters deep at about a seventy-five mile distance point from where we are presently. If the downward grade stays the same, the end of this pipe lies twenty-three miles deep into the earth at its end point. That end point is probably about 2,000 miles west of Baja, California under the Pacific Ocean."

Mike sat down on the ground and just rested his head in his hands. "This is just way too overwhelming. I don't know what to make of this whole project now. The absolute enormity of what we have uncovered goes way beyond any technology or reason for being, than anyone would think possible. My God, what or who built this tunnel? Why here? What could possibly be the objective? I frankly just don't get it, and I don't know how to start to understand this?"

Ike interrupted Mike. "Hey pal, don't panic. We need to explore this thing. There is a purpose here. I for one want to get some answers. I can't let this go."

Mike sharply retorted. "Ike, are you going to take a team of hikers and walk 2,700 miles in the dark with packs of water and food? Give me a break!"

"Look Mike," Ike went on "We can brainstorm this thing. Let's just prop the door open. We'll post guards for the time being, while we figure something out. We all need a rest from this project. We have been at this for over a year and a half. Let's take a breather."

Mike calmed down and returned to Denver. Ike and John shut the pipe project down and posted a few crew to keep any visitors away. It was agreed to next meet in the company's Executive Conference room in about a month. Then everyone would have had time to simply think about this phenomenon and suggest ideas on what the next step should be, if any.

Chapter 16
November 17, 2010

A 10:00 a.m. meeting was scheduled in the Executive Conference room to discuss the pipeline discovery. Attending the meeting were the three principals of the company, Mike, John and Ike.

Mike called the meeting to order. "This is actually Ike's meeting. I don't have any other agenda items to cover other than to comment on our third quarter operations, which were nothing short of sensational. Even after incurring a lot more expense on the Alamogordo and Hagerman pipeline expense adventure, we still had a bottom line for the quarter of over eleven million dollars."

"My turn" said Ike. "The fact that the company is doing so well has a real bearing on what I have to say. As you well know, I have lived this pipeline project more than both of you. If you think I am a little over-consumed with this pipeline mystery, you are absolutely correct. On this matter, I am somewhat possessive and most certainly not objective. This is my baby, and I want to get the answers to why this pipeline exists. I can't let this go, as it now stands."

Ike took a drink of water and continued. "I have really given this matter a lot of deep thought, so here goes. To go twenty seven hundred miles into a black hole would be an extremely perilous undertaking. However, I am willing to risk my life on it to get answers. I don't mean to take foolish risks, however.

I know something must be at the end of the pipeline. Some superior technological organization built this thing, and I am sure they had a purpose. I want to see this through."

John blurted in, "I'm impressed by your ardor, and I for one would gladly support you if going ahead makes sense."

"It does make sense," Ike retorted. At that point, Ike handed out a three page printout listing to Mike and John. "Here is my first pass at brainstorming what I think has to be considered before going forward. I am willing to lead an expedition and take some risks. I feel with careful planning and the right equipment, I have a decent chance of getting to the end of the pipeline and returning."

John broke in again at this point in the meeting. "Look Ike, I'm on your side, but consider this. This pipe was a vacuum chamber for ions before we opened it and exposed it to outside air. To be a vacuum, it would have had to be airtight sealed at the other end. I suspicion you will get to an impenetrable wall at the other end and be able to do nothing but to turn around and head back."

Ike answered right away. "John, I really thought about that a lot. All I can say is maybe knocking on the door at the other end, so to speak, will produce some response or activity. I know it sounds stupid, but I really feel I have to try."

After considering Ike's sincerity, both Mike and John picked up the handouts. Ike went through each item listed under the caption . . . "Requirements For Pipeline Exploration."

Ike began and carefully covered item by item:

1. Three large thirty-two foot long electric carts because we can't have emissions in a closed pipe.
2. Tires on the vehicles that can not go flat.
3. A large compliment of repair parts for the vehicles.
4. Food and water for eight or nine months.
5. Fiber optic cable that can be laid down and serve as communications to the surface.
6. A way to deal with waste, both expended materials and human waste.
7. Medical supplies.
8. A quick method to periodically clean our bodies since there is no way to shower or wash ourselves, plus water is too precious to waste.
9. Many extra batteries for the three vehicles.
10. About one hundred high powered flashlights/and a few lanterns.
11. A communications device to link up with our fiber optic cable.
12. Extra clothing.

Ike read on until forty-six listed items were covered. After finishing the list, he looked up and added. "I am thinking we should have five other men plus myself. I figure we need two persons per vehicle. I also think single men like myself are necessary. Everyone must be in sound physical shape. We can not have anyone who wears glasses or regularly has to take medications. Everyone would need to take a psychological profile exam by a psychiatrist. We don't want anyone getting claustrophobic or freaking out in some other way. We need solidly stable individuals. I figure a minimum of $300,000 per man guaranteed and payable to a beneficiary in one years time if there is no return. Obviously, I don't need the $300,000, so there would only be five payouts. Lastly, everyone who agrees to go has to sign a waiver."

Mike now commented. "As you were going through your list, I was putting an estimated cost for each item. I think the price tag for your list will probably exceed three million dollars. Aside from the money, do you really want to do this Ike? Both of you guys are not only my partners, but also my best friends. I am really out of my comfort zone on this plan!"

"Mike, John," Ike retorted. "Hey I don't want to die either. I really think I can do this and I want to try. Look, think it over and after a week if you guys are okay with this, I will start on my list. Also, if you think of other items to add to my list be my guest."

By the time the meeting broke up, it was almost noon. Mike had arranged for sandwiches and soft drinks for a quick lunch. The general conversation over lunch was light, however, both John and Mike looked over at Ike like they would regret letting a friend involve himself in such a dangerous exploration activity.

A week later, Ike pleaded for and received consents from both of his partners to go ahead. Because of the project, Ike was released from general operations of the firm, so he could fully concentrate on what it would take to get everything ready to begin the tunnel exploration.

Chapter 17
March 15, 2011

Ike picked up the phone on the second ring at his office, "Ike."

Mike started out immediately after Ike answered. "Say Ike, remember those three electric carts you needed for the pipe exploration? Well, look out your window and you will see there are five of those babies sitting in the parking lot. I have been watching them being delivered from my office. Is this a mistake or what?"

"No mistake," Ike answered. "After thinking about the whole situation, I felt we needed to have two chase vehicles to go back in after us if we had an emergency and couldn't use our original three vehicles to get back. The design of the chase vehicles is different than the original exploration vehicles."

"I don't disagree with your logic or the extra expense. Are there any more surprises?" Mike showed some concern in his voice.

"Listen, Mike, if you can drop what you're doing, we can meet in the parking lot. I really want to show you the vehicles." Ike was clearly not put off by Mike's earlier tone of suspicion. Ike remained upbeat and enthusiastic.

In the parking lot, Ike carefully went through the key features of each vehicle. Surprising to Mike was the fact that each thirty-two foot long vehicle had the ability to be operated with either end being the front going forward. Ike explained that this feature was very important in order to return topside. If these long vehicles could not be turned around in the width of the pipe, they could just be driven out which would avoid being permanently stuck in the tunnel. Ike had said that thirty-two feet was not too long to eventually get the vehicle turned with some effort, but he didn't want to take any chances, especially if the pipe got narrower at some point. He strongly felt that if a turn-around failed, they needed to have a vehicle that could go forward from either end.

After hearing the explanation, Mike said, "So how much do each of these giant golf carts cost?"

Ike, with a smile responded. "Because I ordered five at one time, I got the price reduced to $204,000 each."

Mike looked at Ike. "You are definitely not going into our corporate purchasing department. We can't afford you! Seriously, I'm okay with this. Luckily, we can handle all this expense because our general operations are still very profitable. Good profits cover all sins you might say."

At this point, Ike went on about the vehicles and the payload they were designed to carry which included many extra batteries, food, water and a myriad of other items. Ike pulled out a four page printout of all supply items and spare parts that would be loaded on the vehicles.

Ike said "I really did my homework. Several months ago I made a contact at NASA. I talked to the logistics guy. I found out the way they handle food and water plus deal with human waste. We have incorporated all of that into the vehicle supply list here. When you think about it, we have an exploration planned which in concept, is not all that much different than sending a rocket into space. We are lucky however because we don't have air supply or gravity concerns. We calculated what it would take for a seven to eight month operation.

Mike looked at the five vehicles all nicely lined up in the parking lot. "So when do we launch amigo?"

"April 4 is the start date for the trip. I have everything in order. I have carefully screened and chosen our five other volunteers beside myself. I have set up for you and John to meet them next week. Before that meeting, I want to talk to both of you about expectations and some additional logistical details." At that moment Ike asked Mike to go into the driver's cab of one of the lined-up vehicles.

Mike commented and Ike agreed that there was a surprising comfort level in the cab area. Ike demonstrated the fact that all seats fully reclined and could be extended at the bottom to serve as a bed. Mike's countenance showed how he was very impressed with the general design of the cab. Ike further added, "I've really done a lot of research to get to this point and have these vehicles manufactured to my specifications. I'm glad you like what you see so far. By the way, you probably couldn't help but notice that all the vehicles are painted a glossy reflective white. That was done so they would cast off light from the headlights of the vehicle behind. This will help create more light as we venture into the pipe which is going to be pitch black.

Ike turned to Mike. "I'd like to take you for a spin around the parking lot, but I need to get the batteries charged first. How about tomorrow?"

"Okay, Mike answered. "Just let me know when. I'll be in all day."

"Just so you know," Ike said, "the two large carrier vehicles that brought our carts here will be parked at the far end of our parking lot for two weeks. We need them to haul these super carts to Hagerman. We can't drive our electric carts on normal roads."

Both men got out of the drivers cab and walked together around the vehicles several times with Ike pointing out additional features which were not first mentioned, like special tires which can not go flat. After a while both men returned to their respective offices.

Chapter 18
March 29, 2011   10:00 a.m.

The first meeting of the day took place at 10:00 a.m. in the Executive Conference Room. Ike chaired the meeting. Ike painstakingly went over important preliminary details about the planned journey. He covered time lines and communications between the exploration team and topside. These points and others needed to be covered before the 1:30 p.m. meeting where Ike planned to introduce Mike and John to the five volunteers.

Prior to 1:30 p.m. Ike started on his agenda list dealing with the volunteers. "Here is a handout about the five men you will meet this afternoon. All of them are unmarried with no current serious relationships. All of our background checks indicate these men are stable and considered skilled in their selected fields of expertise."

"Here is our doctor. His name is Niles Diamond. I felt we needed a medical presence. He got his MD at Tulane. He finished his general practitioner three year residency last July at a Los Angeles hospital. He answered our ad in a medical journal. He is twenty nine years old. I think Niles is well suited for our mission. He is in excellent health. His parents have passed away and he only has a brother who is in the military. His reason for answering our ad is the guaranteed payment of $300,000 if he was selected and going on our journey. The money is his motivation since medical school has left him with a $200,000 plus debt. Believe me, I made him well aware of the risks. I know you are going to like Niles."

"The next volunteer is a guy named Arnie Salt. He is our mechanic for our electric carts. Again single and not much family. He is thirty years old and from what I gather has a super reputation in his town of Canton, Ohio for mechanical repair work. He owns his own repair business which specializes in automobiles, trucks, golf carts, industrial carts, fork lifts, etc. I explained the nature of what we had manufactured and lent him a set of schematics to study. He feels confident about everything mechanical regarding our vehicle task force. Again, he knows the risks. He says he is a risk-taker and the money he can earn through this adventure will allow him to greatly expand his repair shop back in Canton."

"Now we have Angel Ramirez, whose expertise is the love of hard work and adventure. We had of lot of general purpose applicants to look at. I just really had a good feeling about Angel. He just struck me as a very dependable, rock solid guy who would always be there for us. He is thirty-eight years old. I sort of explained the trip plus the nature of risks. He is really excited about this journey. Angel is from San Diego. He really is aware that there could be some danger, but is very eager to start. Like the others, the offered pay of $300,000 for the trip is a great incentive."

"The fourth guy on the list is Steve Letterman. He is our communications expert. Like the others, he is single. He is thirty-three years old. He signed up early-on and specked-out our fiber optics cable plus all communication devices. He said we paid a fortune but in his opinion we got the best money can buy. He arranged for us to get back-up communications in case some equipment failed. Steve knows what he is getting into. He has a very solid resume and I believe we have a very dependable man here."

"Last of all we have Joe Smith. Pretty ordinary name but I think quite an extraordinary guy. Once you get over the generic name, you will be impressed with Joe. Joe is thirty-five years old. Here goes the history. Joe finished high school at age fourteen. By the time he was twenty one, he attained four graduate majors at the University of Illinois. He holds two PhD's. The one that works for us is the PhD in applied science and engineering from the University of Minnesota. This guy is very technically oriented and we need someone who can make a scientific judgement about what we might encounter at the end of the tunnel. We have to remember, that whoever built this tunnel is way beyond our current technological base. Compared to the human race today, my guess is that the tunnel builders are light years ahead of us. Joe is not an egghead. He is surprisingly affable and gregarious. Joe is currently an instructor on the academic staff at the University of Georgia. He is also a freelance consultant for about three firms in Atlanta. Joe is not married. When I explained to Joe what we found - a twenty seven hundred mile pipeline into the earth, he literally begged to get on board."

"Number six is me. I expect to return. If I don't there is a revised will in an envelope on my desk. So what do you think?"

John sipped some coffee before his reply, "I think you probably picked a good crew. I frankly just worry about this whole thing and the risks. When I think of traveling twenty-seven hundred miles into the earth, I just shudder. I respect you Ike, just think this through a few more times."

"John I appreciate your caution, but I must check this out. I have to dig into this phenomenon. Please understand." With that Ike stood up and went to an easel at the front of the conference room.

Ike turned to a first flip page on the easel. "The next items I need to talk about are very important. As you know the descent grade that we have seen so far is one inch per ten feet. Our biggest risk factors or unknowns is whether the descent factor steepens and/or the tunnel size changes in size or direction. Since we have a good chunk of tunnel to go on, we are banking on no changes in rate of descent, tunnel size and a continued straight direction. With an initial start from our electric cart motors, we can get some momentum and then coast down. The rate of coasting down plus some battery drive propulsion is estimated to be between five to seven miles per hour if we coast most of the way. At that rate of speed with twelve hours of travel per day, it would take us about thirty-eight days to do twenty seven hundred miles. If we get our speed up to an average eight miles per hour and do fourteen hour days we can cut the trip down to about twenty-four days. The question is can we do that speed and still lay the fiber optic communication cable behind us."

"The fiber optic cable is our life-line of communication to the surface. Steve Letterman says he would like to patch the cable to the side of the tunnel at one hundred fifty yard intervals. That would keep it off the floor of the tunnel and we wouldn't run over it on our return trip. Otherwise we were going to just let it spool-out behind the 12 foot diameter spool trailing behind the last of our three vehicles."

"We calculated going at eight miles per hour, stopping every one hundred fifty yards, getting out of the last vehicle to patch the cable to the tunnel wall and getting going again. Since we need thirty seconds to do the cable patch, it slows our rate of speed dramatically because of how many stops we make every one hundred fifty yards. We will try the patch approach at first, but if it is too slow and cumbersome, we will have no choice but to go with plan B and spool out the cable. We are carrying three large spools of cable that can play out for three thousand miles in case our guess of twenty seven hundred miles is short of actual."

"Also on the point of communications. We will have communications monitored topside twenty four/ seven. We plan to call up twice a day at noon and eight p.m. each evening. Further, our topside guy will patch us through to the office or your homes as required if we need to speak with either of you two. So please make sure someone always knows where you both are at all times."

At this juncture in the meeting, John broke in with a question. "Your timeline of twenty-four days to thirty-seven days seems too long. If you would travel for up to sixteen hours per day, you could really cut down on travel time."

"This is a good point about time dedicated to

travel. Everything is a best estimate at this point. Last week I went down to Hagerman. I took two powerful flashlights and walked for thirty minutes into the tunnel. I would say almost two miles. Until you do that little exercise, you have no idea what you are facing. Imagine a pitch black silent darkness except for the lighting you bring with you. Shining a flashlight forward yields nothing until you direct the light beam to a side wall. That means the headlights on the forward cart have to be adjusted to shine more to the left and the right. I also feel the tedium of driving and seeing nothing day after day is going to be a real psychological barrier that we will have to contend with. Maybe sixteen hours per day is possible, but I feel we need more cushion so we have greater periods to relax from this very boring drive."

John responded back to Ike. "I never thought it would be like that. You have really done your homework."

"Just a few more items," Ike went on to say. "We are taking two very high resolution digital cameras that can operate at low light levels. If we come across something interesting, we can get an image and relay it back to the surface. So if we run into a fire-eating dragon, we can share that with both of you."

"I have given you the names of any relationships that are important for contacts with regard to myself and the other five guys. If something does happen, these are the people that will have to be notified."

"For myself, I have asked either Roth Sims or Peter Jenkins in Accounting to go to my house and handle my mail, pay my bills for me and generally check to see everything is okay. They will call you

Mike if there is any problem."

"The flip charts here shows the structural functionality of the vehicles we are taking into the tunnel. I have arrows pointing to food storage, extra batteries, waste containage, extra supplies etc. You need to know what we are dealing with so if we have a fix-it problem we can't solve, you can be of help to us with any ideas." At this point Ike went through three flip pages that had front, side and top views of the travel vehicles.

Ike stepped back from the flip file easel. "I'm done. That's all I have. Unless you have questions let's get a bite to eat before our next meeting this afternoon." Ike quickly sat down.

All three men got up and stretched after relaxing for a moment. They called Mike's secretary who arranged for sandwiches to be brought in along with some cut up fruit and various beverages.

Chapter 19
March 29, 2011 1:30 p.m.

At 1:30 p.m. the conference room doors were opened and five men were marched into the room. They were escorted by Ike's secretary. Handshakes were exchanged along with introductions. All five volunteers had already met each other in the lobby prior to the meeting. Casual conversations ensued for a short ten minutes.

Soon everyone was seated around the massive conference table that took up sixty percent of the space in the Executive Conference Room. Coffee and soft drinks were offered. After everyone was settled in, Mike addressed the group.

"Well first of all, John Nelson and myself are very pleased to meet all of you. You men are going to be a very vital and important team for us. You are all very brave men. I think there will be some astounding discoveries by the time this exploration adventure is concluded. To me personally, this whole things smacks a little like science fiction because we know this tunnel you have heard about, had to be created by a civilization far more scientifically and technologically advanced than what our current civilization represents."

Mike continued. "Your safety and well being is foremost on our minds. We tried to think of every precaution we could take. As you know we even arranged for Dr. Diamond here to be a part of your exploration group."

Niles Diamond interrupted at this point. "Please call me Niles and let's dispense with the doctor title. I'm in this with the rest of you guys. I don't know about the rest of you, but I'm not one for formality." Niles Diamond had a very affectious demeanor and his broad smile made him a welcome friend immediately.

Joe Smith jumped into the conversation next. He was a tall muscular man whose appearance defied what you would expect from a multiple credentialed academic. "As for me, just Joe please. Dr. Smith or Professor Smith just isn't me, okay?"

The group nodded assent to the avoidance of doctor titles. From this time forward it was expected that first names only would apply.

While seated, each man verbally gave a brief "bio" of himself. Following that was a question and answer session with each of the five volunteers asking general questions. Most of the questions were fielded by Ike who was the most responsible for the organizing of the details for the expedition. The most intriguing question came from Angel Ramirez who inquired about rescue plans in case the exploration team needed to be evacuated from the tunnel. Ike responded by telling them that back-up rescue vehicles had been purchased just for that contingency. However, Ike made the following comment. "I must say, however that the distance into the tunnel is significant in terms of hundreds or several thousand miles. Any rescue work to retrieve or help the advance team must be measured in days or weeks. There is risk here and being a volunteer you have to accept a high level of uncertainty as you journey deep within this tunnel."

After the question and answer session, the meeting turned to casual conversation about sports, the economy, regional differences and so on. After about fifteen minutes of small talk, Mike brought the meeting back to order. "Ike tells me we still have quite a bit to do before we begin. John and I will adjourn ourselves now and leave you men with Ike to go over last minute details." As John and Mike left the room, they shook hands all around and told each man how much they respected them and appreciated their willingness to go on this expedition.

Ike continued the meeting with a series of detailed handouts which covered additional preparations each man was expected to complete before the journey began. The meeting finally closed at 3:30 p.m.

Chapter 20
April 4, 2011   8:45 a.m.

Eighteen men gathered at the opening of the tunnel. The night before, the five battery run vehicles arrived in the stealth of the night and were now lined up. Two were parked in reserve with large beige tarps over them to protect the vehicles from the elements plus to conceal them from any aerial or long distance viewing. The other three vehicles formed a line at the tunnel entrance in the order they would proceed into the tunnel.

Five men plus Ike walked around the area taking deep breaths and taking an unprecedented viewing of a deep blue sky. Each took in the luxury of seeing natures beauty unfold with golden brown mountains in the background and a warm sun making its penetration through the expansive sky to once again warm the earth as another day unfolded. As each man walked around, they were silent but sharing the emotions of adventure, fear, being brave, but most of all wondering if they would be entering a tunnel that might ultimately spell their doom and never seeing a blue sky or once again feeling the warmth of the sun on their skin.

Soon there were hugs all around along with handshakes. There was strained laughter and a false sense of joviality that was obviously masking the tension of what was about to occur. Ike finally quieted everyone and it was evident he wished to give a send-off speech. Before Ike began, the silence was profound as a light wind could now be heard as the soft flow of air caressed their presence. "I'm not one for religion, but I would like to offer a quick prayer before we go." At that moment all of the men faced Ike with, most of them, bending their head slightly down and forward in an apparent sign of reverence of what would be said.

"Please God, bless our small group with a good journey and a safe return. We don't know what we face as we enter into this dark unknown. We feel you by our side and have confidence that you will look after us and continually guide us. We trust in you. Amen." Ike looked up as everyone simultaneously did the same.

Mike and John were there for the send-off. Once again, for perhaps the third time that morning, they came over to Ike and gave him bear-like hugs. What was not said was deeply felt.

Now Ike and Arnie Salt went into the front facing cab. The other four men split up into teams of two each going into the front facing cabs of the second and third vehicles. Soon the engines gave out a low pitched hum as they started up and began to inch forward.

It seemed to everyone present, plus the six expedition team members, that they were entering a huge gaping mouth that led them into the earth to be devoured. Within the first minute all three vehicles were inside the tunnel. Viewers that gathered outside the tunnel cold see the headlights being turned on and the ominous lights and shadows being reflected against the black tunnel walls as the procession of vehicles moved forward.

After a few more minutes, there was nothing

more to see if you were standing at the entrance to the tunnel. It was a dark hole reaching into infinity. There was however, the trailing presence of an ultra thin fiber optic cable being spooled off and trailed behind the last vehicle. It was scary to think that this thin line of almost transparent substance was going to be the only lifeline for six brave men.

Chapter 21
April 4, 2011   11:45 a.m.

The travelers had been driving for almost three hours. They had all changed positions with each other and shifted into different vehicles than the ones they used as they originally started forward. All of the men recognized immediately the quick onset of tedium. It was felt that constant changes of vehicles, partners and duties would keep them more awake and alert. They had agreed to stop at noon to get something to eat.

One thing changed after the first hour. It was part of the original plan to stop every one hundred fifty yards to take the fiber optic cable and patch it to a side wall instead of always running it along the floor of the tunnel. It was quickly recognized that doing so was unbelievably time consuming. In order to make any speed at all, the cable was just spooled off behind the last of the three vehicles.

Finally at noon they stopped. Their odometer now showed they had ventured into the tunnel twenty-six miles. Their speed was dictated by how fast they could travel and at the same time, efficiently reel off fiber optic cable.

All the men gathered in the front of the foremost forward vehicle that still had its headlights on. Additionally, several men carried lanterns and as they sauntered forward, eerie shadows moved sinuously along the side walls of the tunnel. Angel Ramirez opened with a comment as each man tore into his assigned lunchtime ration. "Man, this is like the weirdest thing I have ever experienced. Ike, you say this goes for twenty seven hundred miles and this morning we only covered twenty-six? Man that's going to take months to get to the end!"

Ike was quick to jump in because he could see where this line of conversation was heading. "I clocked our rate of speed after we began spooling out cable onto the tunnel floor. We were able to go at about eleven miles per hour after the first hour. If we travel twelve hours per day we could make the distance in about three weeks. However, when you build in tedium, possible maintenance stops, time to communicate topside, I would add another week. I think four weeks would do it. What do you guys think?"

There was a general murmur of agreement and a feeling of acquiesence to accept a short month to make the end.

Ike said, "by the way we have enough water and rations to go between eight and nine months. Also if we needed a chase vehicle rescue, that team would travel at twenty miles per hour to get to us because they wouldn't be burdened by laying cable behind them."

Joe Smith stood up, looked around, and walked over to a side wall of the tunnel. Joe moved his hand slowly along the ultra smooth surface. "This is absolutely amazing. I don't think anyone grasps what the technology must be to create a substance like this and lay a massive pipe structure of this magnitude. This makes the underwater tunnel between England and France look like Legos compared to this. Trust me, there is nothing known on this planet that compares to this."

Ike commented. "Joe, we thought the same when we discovered this tunnel. That's why our company is spending almost eight million dollars so far on this exploration trip. Also, now you know why we have been so secretive about this amazing discovery."

Joe said, "Look at this pipe. There is never the sign of a seam. The width and height don't seem to vary even a centimeter. My God, I'm just in a state of awe."

Niles Diamond went to each man and handed him a multiple day vitamin. "Take this. Our rations don't supply all the vitamins our bodies need. We need to take one of these at lunch each day."

Lunch concluded, and the team decided who would partner-up for each vehicle. After the brief forty-five minute lunch, the journey commenced deeper into the dark tunnel.

Chapter 22
April 8, 2011   8:00 p.m..

As Mike is reading a book in his living room, his wife Ann comes in from the kitchen. "It's another eight o'clock call from Ike." Mike grabs a phone on an end table next to where he was sitting.

"Hi Ike" uttered Mike with an excitement and a happiness that meant another routine call is a good sign all is well.

"Mr. Dennis, this is Dan Arky at the tunnel entrance. Please wait a few seconds so I can put Ike Tenner through to you."

There is about twenty seconds of silence and then a little burst of static. "Mike, are you on?" It was Ike's voice and the connection seemed very good tonight.

"Mike, I've got to tell you, this is much harder than I thought. Being in constant darkness in a never ending tunnel really gets to you. All of us have to pep each other up."

"It's not hard to fall into a depressed state of mind. We literally can't wait until we can eat or sleep. The tedium is overwhelming. You know, the person who stays upbeat is Joe Smith. He is so excited to get to the other end and see what can be discovered. He's our cheerleader and God knows we need one. All is going well. We try not to get on each other's nerves and bicker. Our odometer has us at five hundred twenty eight miles so far. I would say we are at the twenty percent mark.

"Oh one thing you should know Mike. Our beginning grade of descent was one inch per ten feet. The grade has now slightly steepened to one and a quarter inches per ten feet. That's actually a big deal as our vehicles can roll down just slightly faster than before and save on our battery. The downside, excuse the pun, is that our return trip will be a little harder going uphill. Not to worry at this point."

"Hey Ike," Mike said rather passively, "Are you still okay with this?"

"Yeah, I'm okay. But its really hard on us. I'll sign off for now. Take care Mike. Good bye."

"Good bye" Mike answered not sure whether Ike was still on the line to hear him. Every time he heard Ike say "good bye" it seemed so final and it scared him. Mike put the phone down and picked up his book.

Chapter 23
April 14, 2011   3:00 p.m.

The procession of vehicles suddenly stopped when the forward vehicle came to an abrupt halt. The four men in vehicles two and three got out of their cabs and walked forward carrying their flashlights. When they were along side of the first cab, they opened the cab door. Niles and Angel were calmly sitting in the first cab.

Ike said, "Why did you stop?"

Angel was quick to answer with a shrug. "I think our battery is gone and needs to be recharged. Let's test it."

The battery was pulled out and tested. Sure enough, it was dead. This would be their third battery change since they began their journey. Now they were experienced in such maintenance issues. They found it took twelve minutes on average to change over the batteries and put an old battery on recharge.

It was ten days now. For the most part, any pair of two men in a cab were generally silent while one drove and the other daydreamed, slept or read a book. Everyone had already been paired up numerous times. Their previous conversations had by and large covered the history and experiences of each traveler. Often the silence as they drove, was a product of nothing new to talk about.

Chapter 24
April 17, 2011   8:03 p.m.

Mike picked up the telephone at home on the first ring. "Mike here."

The caller did not identify himself and only said, "Hold please for Ike."

"Mike?" Ike asked inquisitively.

"Yes, Ike, I'm here. Day fourteen, right?" Mike cradled the phone between his shoulder and neck as he reached for his notepad.

"Right on." Ike was quick to answer. "We are now sixteen hundred ten miles into the tunnel. I feel like I have been doing this for months. This is the toughest thing in my mind that I have ever done. My thoughts go from, is it worth it, might I end up dying down here, are we prepared for what we might encounter, etc. All of us have the same haunts. Talking to you each night is more therapeutic than you will ever know."

"First of all we are making a little better time this past two days. I will tell you, we are a silent group now. We seem to be somewhat "small talked" out as we have had everyone as a cab buddy back and forth many times. I can almost tell you verbatim what medical school was like for Niles, or how to fix a car from Arnie. When we get done, any of these guys will know as much about mining operations as I know."

"Actually there is nothing really new to report. We found two dead birds today. They probably got sucked in when we allowed air in to fill the vacuum after the tunnel door was opened. I was really not surprised. Who knows what all got sucked in? I'm just glad it wasn't us."

"Overall, we are doing as well as can be expected. Hopefully in ten to twelve days we arrive at our destination whatever that will be. You would laugh at the speculation that goes on here about what lies at the end of our journey."

"Ike, I'm glad everything is still going okay." Mike's relaxed state came through to Ike as he continued to converse. "I really look forward to your calls. John and I really miss you. Just so you know, we hit a motherload on that new mine in Utah. Now we can afford your extravagance."

"Hey, Mike, it's all about the money, isn't it?" Ike chuckled. "We're just a return on investment fodder."

"No Ike, of course not. John and I really like you. But if you bring back diamonds or uranium, we would like you much better!" Mike's laugh at the end was genuine and warm.

"Okay wise guy" Ike retorted in a sarcastic tone. "I'll say good-bye. You know where you can find us."

"By the way one more thing before I hang up," Ike added. "You know I brought my portable computer so I could keep a diary of our journey. I have not started yet because every day is so boring. Once we get to the end of the tunnel, I will start so we have a detailed documentary of what we find."

They each said good-bye again.

As per usual the following day witnessed Mike

calling John and telling him about Ike's phone call and progress-to-date.

Chapter 25
April 24, 2011   8:04 p.m.

The connection had already been made as Ike began bringing Mike up to date on progress. "We are in twenty four hundred fifty miles as of tonight. It's funny to say tonight, because it is night all the time for us. Our vehicles are still working great. Our morale is picking up because we feel we are only three to four days away from where we estimated an ending to the tunnel."

"Mike, we get more tired now at the end of each day. The continued darkness and nothingness ahead of us is really playing havoc with our minds."

"Ike," Mike broke in, "Just hang in there buddy. Remember, we need the diamonds and the uranium!"

"Sure thing Mike. What should I pick from the pile, white diamonds or blue diamonds?" Ike was spirited in his retort.

"Blue, by all mean." Mike chuckled again.

"Okay, blue it will be. Say hi to John. Got to go now. I have a heavy date with my pillow. Talk to you tomorrow. Bye."

Chapter 26
April 27, 2011   4:15 p.m.

Topside, Dick Pierce took the call at the entrance to the tunnel. He patched the call through to Mike's office only to find he had an appointment out of the building. Next Ike tried to call John. It took a while to find John who finally answered a general page. John picked up the phone in a nearby conference room.

"John Nelson here."

"John, it's Ike. Good to talk to you again. I tried Mike first but he is evidently not in the building. John, we did it!! We got to the end of the tunnel. It's twenty eight hundred and two miles. By God we made it!!"

"Hey Ike, Mike told me you were going to return with diamonds. Good man!" John remarked.

"Right!" Ike answered. "Listen, I have to tell you the end of the tunnel is very unusual. We need to explore a little. Tell Mike I will call him around 8:00 p.m. tonight as usual. I've got to go now. Bye."

Chapter 27
April 27, 2011   8:10 p.m.

Mike answered the telephone after hearing the very first ring. He was laying on the couch with the phone in his lap waiting to click "talk." Mike had been anxiously waiting for this call for at least twenty minutes.

"Mike here, are you on the phone now Ike?"

"Yes Mike," Ike answered. "I'm on and happy to say we reached the tunnel's end. We have been resting up and celebrated with a bottle of champagne I brought along for this final occasion. We have been exploring around for a while. So here goes."

"For the last mile before the end of the tunnel, we counted forty six two foot diameter circular vents in the side walls. This is obviously how someone extracted air from the tunnel and created a vacuum chamber. Imagine the power it took to suck all the air out of this vast tunnel."

"You will find this particularly interesting. The very end seems to have a door, but very different from the one topside. The end here is formed by what looks like about eighty triangular pieces all formed together and interconnected. Again it seems like these triangular pieces are made of the same substance as the tunnel."

"So far there is no sign of life or anything around that would seem to allow us to get the door open. We put our ears to the door and Niles Diamond's stethoscope, but hear nothing at all."

Mike commented back. "Why don't you take a wrench or a heavy metal object and slam on the door and see if you get any reaction?"

Ike laughed. "Sure we'll try your suggestion since we can't seem to find a doorbell."

"Hi Mike, I'm back on," Ike said. "Angel is banging on the door now. I have to say this really seems like a stupid way to announce ourselves."

Ike and Mike converse for a couple of minutes while Angel is joined by Arnie who is also wielding a long metal object. Both men are now clanging objects against the end door.

"Mike, I'm getting a headache from this noise. We can't keep this up much longer. Oh shit! The door looks like it's moving. There is a bit of light coming from a one inch hole opened up in the center. Holy shit! The door opens from the center and the area of opening is getting larger."

"Oh my God, there is something moving on the other side of the door but we can't make it out. Mike, there is somebody home here. Mike, I'll call you back in a few minutes. I've got to get up to the door with the other guys. This is unbelievable!"

Mike heard the phone go silent. There was never another call back that night. That was the last communication. Attempts topside to reach any of the six explorers were never answered.

Chapter 28
May 10, 2011   10:15 a.m.

John, unannounced walks into Mike's office and with some sense of urgency closes the door loudly behind him. As Mike somewhat startled looks up, John abruptly sits down in a chair across from Mike. "It's been almost two weeks and not a word. Don't you think we should send a chase team down to check on what happened? That's why we bought those extra two vehicles!"

"John, please just calm down for a second." Mike tried to be relaxed when he responded. This was the second time in two weeks John panicked at the time that had gone by with no communication. "Let's just think this through before we do something we will forever regret. Remember any team we send will be less trained and more at risk than the first team. Sending another vehicle down will trample the cable we depend on for communication, so there would be no communication from the first team or the second team. It took our exploration team almost a month to traverse the tunnel. It would take three more weeks for them to even return assuming they came back immediately. Listen I have given this a lot more thought than you give me credit for. Remember, Ike suggested waiting at least six months to send a second team down if we lost communication. That's just what we need to do."

"Mike, I just don't like it. I hear you but it pains me to just sit around for months and do nothing." John's voice was much calmer.

"John," said Mike. "There is something you can do. Search out a prospective group of volunteers that would be ready to go after six months. Get provisions for the rescue vehicles. That would help if the time came where we would send an emergency team into the tunnel."

"Okay, I'll get on it. I'm just really, really, worried."

"So am I." Mike responded quickly as he got up from his chair and came around to where John was getting up to go. "John, I still have faith everything will be okay."

Chapter 29
October 10, 2011

It was the normal Monday morning 9:30 a.m. review meeting held in Mike Dennis's office. This time the only attendees were Mike and John Nelson. After about thirty minutes of each updating the other on the status of projects, there was an unusual silence finally punctuated by John Nelson.

"Mike," uttered John. "It has been almost six months and not a word from Ike or any of the rest of the group. I think we need to do something, don't you?"

"John, I know just how you feel." Mike poured himself some coffee as he continued to speak. "I think about this situation almost every hour of every day. Every time I think of sending a back-up team in our second group of vehicles, I cringe. I fear sending four more volunteers to their death and still maybe never knowing what happened. You know, we are getting a few calls from some family members of our first team and it is hard to put them off very much longer. This is a real dilemma and I just don't know what we should do."

"Mike," John quickly answered. "I also think about Ike all the time. Just like you, I need to have feedback on what happened but I am also reluctant to put more people at risk."

Mike got up from his chair and walked over to his office window and looked out. It was a beautiful clear blue sky with the sun shining brightly. He thought about Ike and his exploration group having been denied sunshine and outside air for over six months. Other thoughts began to plague his mind as he spoke. "Let's give it another few weeks. If still no word, we will ready our rescue team to go in. However, I don't think we can take full responsibility at this point. If a rescue mission is initiated, I think we need to get a government agency involved. I don't see any other choice from a liability perspective. Any agency would take over and of course we would lose control on this whole project. In fact, an agency may overrule our selection of volunteers for a rescue team and send in others they would select. Maybe, I think that would be best so any adversity or loss of lives would not be fully on our conscience."

John stood up and walked over to the window by Mike. "Let me think your ideas through. Right now it sounds like your approach is the best way to deal with a really awful situation. I think we need to contact our attorney and bring him up to speed before we divulge anything to a government agency."

Chapter 30
October 14, 2011

At mid-afternoon the telephone rings in John Nelson's office. The caller is Todd Mason who is one of four sentries standing vigil at the tunnel entrance. Casually John picks up the phone. "John Nelson speaking."

Todd Mason with a hurried clip of speech shouted into the phone. "We got contact with the group. Steve Letterman got on the line and said they were heading back today. They said they aren't sure how long the trip will take but they are starting back. He said they will try and call every other day on their way back. They are only taking two vehicles back. He said they were very sorry to inform everyone at the company that there are only four people returning. He said Ike Tenner and Joe Smith died. Steve Letterman did not give any explanation as to how they died or when. That was all there was when they ended the call. Mr. Nelson, I'm calling you because when I called for Mr. Dennis, his secretary said he wasn't in the office so the call was transferred to you."

John Nelson was stunned at the thought of his partner Ike having died. He was visibly shaking as he simply ended the telephone call with "Thank you, Todd, just please make sure Mike or I are called if there is any additional contact."

After the call, John had Mike paged. After a few minutes, Mike called John's extension. "Hey John, what's up?"

John answered in a very worried solemn tone. "Can you come to my office Mike? We need to talk now. This is very urgent and I don't want to cover what I have to say over the telephone."

"Okay," Mike replied. "I'll be over to your office in just a minute or two, bye."

Without knocking, Mike entered John's office and sat down on his couch at the opposite corner from John's desk. "John, you look like some really bad news is coming. What's wrong?"

"Ike is dead." John slowly uttered those words with a profound unsteadiness to his voice.

"Oh my God! What happened?" Mike's tone was clearly evident of his being totally unnerved at the mention of Ike's demise.

John Nelson walked over to a chair near the couch where Mike sat. As John sat down, he began to recite what he had been told. "I just got a call put through to me from Todd Mason at the tunnel. Todd said he had just received a call from Steve Letterman. Steve told him that they are beginning their return trip in two vehicles. He said there are only four people returning. Letterman told Mason that Ike Nelson and Joe Smith died. It seems that Letterman did not give any particulars about what has happened for six months or anything at all about the two deaths."

Both men just quietly stared at each other for several minutes without speaking. Mike broke the silence. "I'll call Todd and ask if any more calls come in from anyone in the returning group, those calls need to be patched through directly to you or me

99

immediately. I don't want any second-hand information. Let's make sure someone always knows where we both are day or night." At that point Mike got up quietly and walked out of John's office and into his own office down the hall. On his way into his office, Mike Dennis told his secretary to cancel any meetings for the day.

At midnight, Mike Dennis was startled as he was sharply awakened at his home when the phone rang at his bedside. He groped for the phone and picked up. "Yes, Mike Dennis."

"Hold Mike, this is Jim Sparks at the tunnel. I am putting through Steve Letterman. Here's Steve."

"Is this Mike Dennis?" Steve Letterman's voice was surprisingly placid.

"Yes Steve, this is Mike. What happened? How did Ike and Joe die? What's been going on down there for six months and not a word of communication?"

"Mike, I honestly am a little vague as to how Ike and Joe died. I just sort of remember some sort of accident and our medical guy Dr. Diamond saying they had expired. Also, I didn't know we were down here for six months. It has only seemed like a few weeks or so to all of us. We really didn't discover anything at all. I also am not sure why we have not called before our decision to return topside."

"What the hell kind of response or report is that?" Mike was livid and the irritation he was feeling was very much clear in his sharpened rhetoric to Letterman. "You've told me nothing. Surely something occurred. Ike's last message to me was that the end of the tunnel was opening up and light was filtering in from the other side of a doorway. So what was that all about? What kind of accident happened and how long ago?"

"Mike, I know you're angry. I can hear it in your tone of voice." Steve Letterman continued unrealistically calm and monotone as he continued. "I honestly don't remember more than I told you. I just don't really remember what happened to Ike and Joe. We just all want to get back. Here, I'll let you talk to Niles."

Dr. Niles Diamond was given the telephone. "This is Niles, Mike. I wish I could tell you more than Steve did. I remember pronouncing Ike and Joe dead but I draw a blank when I try to recall how they died. I can't seem to focus on what happened. Also, I can't even remember what we did with the bodies before we left."

Mike was silent for a few seconds. "Niles, do any of the four of you remember anything at all. My God man, your team has been gone for six months with not a damn call back to us. What the hell is going on! Surely you have to know something. If I were to ask Angel Ramirez or Arnie Salt these obvious questions, would I still get the same unacceptable vague answers?"

"Yes Mike," continued Diamond. "We have all talked about this journey before we called tonight. For some reason we just don't remember much at all and none of us felt we were here for as long as six months."

Mike finished off the call with an exasperated sigh. "Just get back safely. Keep calling regularly and if anyone remembers anything, call me right away please." Mike hung up the phone. He waited a few minutes to contain his anger before calling John Nelson.

It was shortly after midnight, when John Nelson was awakened by the call from Mike. As soon as he heard Mike's voice, he was alerted to the level of venting that would occur as Mike needed to share his concerns about the entire tunnel exploration project.

Chapter 31
November 11, 2011

The return trip lasted twenty nine days. There continued to be a daily phone call from Steve Letterman giving a return trip progress report. Besides the basic report, no additional details came forth as to what happened during the six months they were gone after reaching the end of the tunnel.

At 9:00 p.m. Mike Dennis took a call at home from Todd Mason who was on duty at the tunnel. "Mike, this is Todd They're back! They look absolutely exhausted and disheveled. Otherwise they seem okay. At your request they will be held here to be examined by the doctor you said would be sent after they returned. I told them they need to have physical exams to see if they were really okay. They were okay with that but just wanted to get showered and get a decent night's sleep. They are in our portable now getting cleaned up. What do we do with them next?"

"Todd" Mike answered. "After they clean up and change clothes, get them to a local motel. Use discretion on checking them in. Also get them some decent food. Don't take them to a restaurant. Have them eat on site. I want them not to be exposed to anyone until they are checked out medically."

"Also, as soon as everything checks out, get these men transportation back to Denver, our office specifically. Please call my secretary and set up a meeting for all these guys to be in our executive conference room. After these men are sent off, please close up the area with a barricade blocking the tunnel entrance. For all of you who have stood guard at the tunnel entrance, take a two week paid extra vacation on the company and have a good Thanksgiving."

After the phone call, Mike telephoned John Nelson and informed him that the tunnel expedition team had returned. He explained the medical exam precaution. He asked John to keep his calendar relatively clear so a meeting can be held as soon as the expedition team returned to Denver. Mike also asked John, "John, what do you feel about my hunting up a highly regarded psychiatrist and have the doctor attend the meeting. These guys are acting very peculiar with their memory loss and seeming not to know they were gone for months. These guys aren't right! I will pay what it takes to get a psychiatrist to break his appointment schedule and attend the meeting. I know of two docs that have a solid reputation. What do you think of this idea?"

John quickly answered. "You actually suggested it before I could. These guys really seem off balance. Not only should the doctor be at the meeting but I would like to have him have one on one sessions with each man. We will have to meet with the doctor before he comes, to bring him up to speed on the tunnel project and the entire exploration trip. Medical professionals must keep all matters confidential.

Chapter 32
November 15, 2011

At 9:00 a.m., the doctor was announced by Mike's secretary. After the doctor (William Rutherford) was seated at the couch in Mike's office, John Nelson ushered himself into Mike's office and sat in a chair adjacent to Dr. Rutherford. Mike sat down with them as introductions and some small talk was mutually exchanged. Mike thanked Dr. Rutherford for changing his appointment schedule around to accommodate the needs of Mike and John's corporation.

Mike with notes in hand, spent considerable time covering the project and what seems to have occurred with the expedition team returning. Mike was very emotional when he talked about the announced death of his partner and Joe Smith. Mike was very concerned that there was some "cover-up" of what might have happened since the return team seemed to be rather non-chalant about the tragedy plus chalking up memory loss as an explanation for lack of details. "Dr. Rutherford, these guys are concealing information about what happened. They were gone for six months and never a phone call. They seem very unwilling to go into any details. They just say they can't remember, and worst of all they think that answer is acceptable."

Mike continued. "Doctor, we are going to introduce you as a medical doctor when you attend our meeting. I will not go into specifics about you're being a psychiatrist, because I don't want these men spooked.

I think it best if you listen but don't contribute at the meeting. How do you feel about that approach?"

"Well first of all," Dr. Rutherford said, "I am amazed at the idea of a tunnel going so deep into the earth. I appreciate your bringing me into your confidence, which I assure you will be kept. I think just listening at the meeting is the best way to start. After the meeting I will be glad to meet with you both and give you a preliminary diagnosis or judgement statement. Also I have cleared my calendar for today and tomorrow to meet with each of these four men."

Mike got up. "It's about 10:00 a.m. and we all need to go to the conference room where I believe these four men are waiting for us."

Actually Mike, John, and Dr. Rutherford got to the conference room before anyone else. Within a minute of their arrival, Mike's secretary brought the four men into the conference room. Mike, John and Dr. Rutherford were already seated with coffee mugs in front of them. Very quickly the four adventurers were seated, with Mike introducing Dr. Rutherford as a physician but being deliberately vague as to why he was attending.

Mike and John had a pre-typed list of subjects and questions for the meeting. It was decided that John Nelson would start as the four men knew less of his role in the company and might be more relaxed with his management of all questions.

John started out slowly with a smile on his face in order to convey a welcome environment for the meeting as opposed to an inquisition tone. "Fellas, we are really glad that you are back safely. We know from conversations with Ike when you were going deeper into tunnel, that this was a far more arduous journey than we expected. We are just really glad you are back. Obviously we are saddened that our best friend Ike and Joe Smith died. Later in the meeting we have some questions about what happened. However, I will put those questions off for now. So welcome back."

This was a cordial start, and Dr. Rutherford saw the body language of these four men as they seemed a little more at ease.

It was decided to go around the table with each man taking a turn in telling about the journey from his own personal perspective. It was apparent at the end of all the commentary, that this had been a terrible ordeal and everyone was grateful to be back above ground.

John sat straight in his chair and delivered his first question. "I want to start out with how you felt and what you saw when you first realized you had reached the tunnel ending. Let's go in order of how you are seated at the conference table. Angel first, then Steve, then Niles and finally Arnie. So Angel, tell us what you saw and how you felt about what you witnessed?"

Angel along with the other three covered in detail the hour that they stopped at the end of the tunnel. They described the tunnel end as a solid wall or closure which was made of the same impenetrable materials as the walls of the tunnel. They were fairly placid in their statements that there was nothing more to talk about. The tunnel ended without any discovery.

John then went into his next question. "You know, Ike was in communication with us for a brief time when you reached the tunnel end point. His initial statements were exactly the same as your recollections of what you each saw. Ike said that some of you were banging on the end surface with metal objects to get some attention even though he remarked that it seemed like a dumb thing to do. However, there was an interesting point as Ike said something before he signed off the call. Ike said and I am repeating his words exactly." At this point John looked down at his notes. "Oh shit, the door looks like it is moving. There is a bit of light coming from what is looking like a small hole in the center of the end wall. Holy shit, it opens from the center and the area of opening is getting bigger. Oh my God, there is something on the other side but I can't make it out from here. Mike, there is somebody home here. Mike, I'll call you right back. I've got to get up to the door with the other guys. This is unbelievable!"

John looked up from his notes. "To me, Ike was witnessing something he viewed as spectacular. Angel, does this bring back anything to you as to what you personally saw?"

Angel looked at his three travel companions and then back to John. "No, I'm sure that didn't happen. I would not forget something like that."

At that point in the meeting, Steve, Nile and Arnie had incredulous looks and almost uttered in unison that the tunnel came to an end with no opening whatsoever. As Dr. Rutherford observed, each man's expressions were adamant in their belief that Ike's comments were a complete fabrication.

It was apparent that emotions were rising quickly at the meeting and John Nelson immediately went on to another question. "Okay, let's move on. When we outfitted the three vehicles, we put on board enough rations and water that if carefully managed would last eight to nine months for six men. Upon your return all of the rations in your vehicle were at initial levels except for what four men would consume over a two month period which would coincide with a round trip only. Since rations were equalized for each vehicle there would not have been enough food and water consumed to sustain four to six men for the downward journey and return trip plus a stay of six months. Our question is how could you survive with the small amount of rations that were actual consumed?"

Steve with an expression of anger answered. "Mr. Nelson, we felt like we were only down at the tunnel end for maybe ten days - two weeks tops. We ate our rations and drank water every night. We just were not gone for eight months including travel time in the tunnel."

Mike jumped in the conversation. "Do you all agree that you started the journey down on April 4, 2011?"

The four men all responded yes.

Mike continued. "When you came back you were handed a Denver newspaper to catch up on news. That newspaper is here and has a date of November 11, 2011. So how does that square with only being in the tunnel for travel time down and back plus two weeks?"

Niles spoke up. "I don't know what to tell you. We honestly feel like we were at the end of the tunnel for less than two weeks. We can't explain the six months being at the end of the tunnel. The truth for us is a ten day to two week memory. I can't explain the surplus food inventory or the newspaper date."

Arnie Salt and Steve Letterman were vehement in their agreement with Niles Diamond. They both showed on their countenance that they were extremely incensed about the inference that the whole truth was not being told.

Quickly Mike Dennis spoke up. "Gentlemen this is not an inquisition. We only want to know what your experiences were like in the tunnel. Let's end this part of our questions dealing with time intervals. We accept that the four of you concur that you were only in the tunnel for about two and one half months."

Mike Dennis then put out innocuous questions dealing with the journey. Such questions dealt with fears, darkness, ability to get along, problems encountered, etc. These less threatening questions were more calmly answered and the high emotions of earlier were diffused considerably.

At a calmer point in the meeting, John Nelson took over once more. "My next question is to Dr. Niles Diamond. I assume you medically attended to Ike Tenner and Joe Smith. What in your opinion caused their death?"

Niles Diamond with a somewhat stupefied look, just shrugged his shoulders in answering. "I am ashamed to say as a medical doctor that I just don't know. Somehow I know I checked over the bodies and pronounced them both deceased. I just can't recall any more than that. I knew this question would be asked of me. I have struggled with my lack of memory on this issue and I just can't seem to remember anything of relevance. I can't even recall what we did with the dead bodies. I know we couldn't bring them back because of the decay factor, so I think we just had to leave our two dead friends at the tunnel end-point."

After Dr. Diamond spoke, an abject silence pervaded the meeting room. Dr. Rutherford took note of the expressions on the faces of each of the four men. He jotted down quick notations on a pad but continued to say nothing at the meeting.

There were a few more simpler questions from John Nelson over the next twenty minutes.

The meeting was concluded at 12:15 p.m. Mike Dennis echoed the following summary comments to the four men as a group. "First of all, we are appreciative of your having volunteered for what was a very arduous adventure with an uncertain outcome. We are glad the four of you returned safely. We promised each of you a $300,000 payment upon your return. On Friday, the eighteenth of November, your checks less mandatory tax withholding will be waiting for you at my secretary's office."

Mike took a drink of water and then continued. "However, there is an interim request. I would ask each of you to meet in a private session with Dr. Rutherford during either today, tomorrow or Thursday." Mike pointed to Dr. Rutherford who smiled and nodded.

"Also," Mike continued. "I would like each of you to give us a contact telephone number so we can talk to you in the future if something comes up where we need more information. In closing, I wish you well and also a Happy Thanksgiving next week."

After the four men filed out of the room, Mike Dennis, John Nelson and Dr. Rutherford remained seated.

"Mike and John" answered Dr. Rutherford, "I really can't give you a good response at this point. It seemed to me that these men gave what they thought were honest answers. Yet it was obvious to everyone here that their answers didn't agree with the facts or an expected more reasonable response. I really did not detect any collusion here. As we agreed earlier, let me meet with all of these men in one-on-one private sessions. After I have met with everyone, I can meet with both of you on Friday. My meeting with Dr. Diamond should prove particularly revealing."

Chapter 33
November 18, 2011

Dr. Rutherford was escorted into Mike's office by Mike's secretary. John Nelson had arrived earlier and was already seated. Handshakes were extended and coffee and soft drinks were set on a large coffee table where the three men were seated.

Mike started out. "Dr. Rutherford, did you have enough opportunity to meet with all four men?"

"Yes Mike," Dr. Rutherford replied. "I did. I found the meetings with these men very productive. When I say productive, I speak from a psychiatric standpoint as opposed to getting better answers then you initially received at the group meeting earlier this week."

Dr. Rutherford opened a notebook in front of him and regularly looked down at the book as he addressed Mike and John. "From the standpoint of honesty, each man is telling the truth as he knows it. Their stories agree to each other even though what they say is at variance with the facts at hand or even simple logic."

"From the standpoint of psychiatry, all these men are jointly suffering from 'disassociative amnesia.' This is not uncommon to see in any patient when there has been a severe trauma or a personal catastrophe. It is extremely unusual to have a group of people witness the same earthshaking event and all form the identical pattern of amnesia. This is the first time that I have ever encountered this malady on a group basis. I did a little research and discovered where war-time episodes were experienced, it was reported that group amnesia effects existed for several men at the same time, but never all the troops."

"I found it most interesting that the selective amnesia that I witnessed in these men almost has a surgical precision to it with respect to what each man remembered and what information or memory was lost. If I were to go to an extreme here, it was like each man was brainwashed or trained to respond in a certain way. Before the journey and afterward, their mental capacities and memories are excellent. I can't prove it, but it seems like these men were taught what to forget."

Dr. Rutherford discussed further other types of psychiatric phenomenon which he had gathered from his recent research efforts. He cited documentation about brainwashing and prisoner of war experiences.

After a while Mike and John were growing a little weary of the various medical implications and sought a convenient time to adjourn the meeting.

Mike sort of finalized their feelings to Dr. Rutherford. "So basically," Mike said "these guys believe they are telling the truth even though some of it does not make sense and their hiding behind memory lapses is the best we get. There are two dead men who have not returned and we have to be satisfied with their shoulder shrug of not remembering anything. Is that about it?"

Dr. Rutherford retorted quickly. "I would hate to state the situation in such an angry demeanor, but yes that's about all we are going to get. I could always go the route of some truth serums but you get into major liability issues with that and run up against a myriad of patient rights which would be violated. Frankly, I tried, but there does not seem to be much left open to us. I'm sorry I couldn't help get some more definitive answers."

About ten minutes after Dr. Rutherford and John Nelson departed Mike's office, Mike's secretary came in carrying a small package.

"Mr. Dennis," the secretary began, "Steve Letterman came to my office a short while ago to pick up his check prior to leaving for the airport. He told me he woke up this morning and suddenly remembered something important. He recalls rather vaguely that before Ike Tenner died, he was asked by Ike to personally deliver this package to you. He told me he couldn't remember this earlier at the Monday meeting and it just seemed to pop into his head when he woke up today."

Mike took the package and thanked his secretary. The package was square about eight inches long by eight inches wide tied together with string. It was about three inches thick and seemed to weigh very little. The package was wrapped with a shiny silvery blue material similar to foil but much smoother with a silk cloth feel. On the package was a note in Ike's handwriting. The note said the package must be opened by either Mike Dennis or John Nelson personally.

Mike picked up the phone and asked John to drop whatever he was doing and come to Mike's office. After John arrived, he was handed the package and told what Mike's secretary had stated earlier. Both men handed the package back and forth to each other while confirming Ike's handwriting. Both men showed hesitancy about opening the package.

Chapter 34
November 18, 2011

After a few more back-and-forths with the package and feeling the silky silvery blue covering, John was the first to comment. "Let's open this up." At that point John pulled at the string tied with a bow and quickly unwrapped the package. Inside he found three computer disks and a folded handwritten note from Ike. He put the disks on Mike's desk and handed the note to Mike. He then took the note back and read it aloud.

"Dear John or Mike: I don't quite know where to begin. As you see there are three CD's in the package. Please print out CD marked #1 first. Do this first. This is not for your secretary or anyone else to read. This information is only for John Nelson or Mike. Dennis."

Mike went over to his closet. "John, doesn't Ike have the same personal computer as we do? I think we bought all three together last year." Mike put his portable computer on his desk. He plugged it in and also connected it to his printer on an adjacent credenza. After the computer was warmed up and the printer turned on, Mike inserted disk number one. He quickly pushed the print button when the proper icons showed up on his computer screen. Both men waited while the printer engaged.

There was a silence and then a hum as the disk

message was being printed out. Three double spaced pages spilled out of the printer. Mike grabbed the three pages quickly. "John let's sit down over on the sofa and we will read together what this says."

Dear Mike and John: First of all let me start out by telling you now that Joe Smith and I are alive. What you were told about our deaths was not true, although the other four men who told you we had died honestly thought they were being truthful. More, later on disk two, about the misinformation about our demise. Do not worry about Joe and I. We are very much alive and well. As you can imagine we have information to divulge to you two which will be shocking beyond your wildest imagination. Again, let me address all of that in disk two.

We will not be returning for a long time. There is a slight chance we may decide not to ever return. In the meantime you need to take personal and legal steps to deal with explaining our prolonged disappearance.

First of all we need to deal with Joe Smith. Fortunately Joe is single. Both of his parents are deceased. He has one sister who you will need to contact. After you have read the contents of disc one and two, you will be in a position to handle what needs to be said. She needs to hear this from you in person, so please arrange for her to come to Denver. Since she is the only one important to Joe, his assets need to go to his sister with the idea as

if he never returned from the tunnel journey and is presumed dead. Make sure Joe's sister gets the $300,000 payment due to Joe. Joe sends his love and wishes you to tell his sister that he may some day come back and to not despair for the years of separation or possibility of not returning ever. This of course seems easier said than done. However, once she is told the truth about what has happened, Joe knows she will understand.

As for me I have a mother living and I have two brothers. This may or may not be easier since you and John know my family quite well. Please call all of them to your office personally when you cover what is happening to me. Because years will go by before I might consider returning, you need to take different steps for me. I want all my assets to go into a trust set up by Attorney McCarthy. I guess you will need to trust him with the truth about our journey in order for him to understand what is happening. Between both of you and McCarthy, use your judgement about handling my personal assets, share of the business, tax returns, etc.

Now a quick synopsis of what is really going on down here. There is an end to the tunnel. As crazy as it sounds, there is an active thriving civilization here with technological advances far beyond our comprehension.

Disk two will give you a very detailed almost daily account of our six months with these people who make up this astounding civilization. They let me keep my personal computer which I brought down and are extremely trusting that my best friends will honor the sanctity of information that I will share with you.

I promised my new friends here that shortly after the four others returned, you would seal off the tunnel. Please remove all evidence of our presence at the mouth of the tunnel. Close the tunnel door so that the vacuum chamber can be restored. It is vitally important that there are no more ventures into the tunnel. You will understand why after reading the printout from the contents of disc two.

There is a possibility of Joe and I returning without going through the tunnel. This civilization has an escape route that lies about twenty miles below the floor of the Pacific Ocean, which as you know is directly above us. Again I don't know if we will return or not. If five years go by and we have not returned, assume we will live out our lives here.

Tell my family that I love them and to trust that I am doing the right thing. Both of you two have always been my best friends. I know I can rely on you to manage what you are about to learn. Ike Tenner.

Chapter 35
November 18, 2011

After Mike finished reading the letter aloud, he had a look of total bewilderment. Mike started to say something and then stopped and just silently looked at John for some reaction. Mike continued to silently stare at John as if he were frozen in some stupefied trance.

John was first to speak. "Mike if this is true and we have no reason to believe it isn't, this is a discovery and responsibility that is likely greater than has ever occurred before. I am stunned at what Ike said in his message. I don't even know where to begin. My mind is awash with question after question. My first question is why didn't the four guys who came back say something about this. This is not like some trivial thing one forgets."

Mike walked over to the credenza behind his desk. "John, I'm putting disc number two in now and get it printed out." Mike went and took out disc one and quickly inserted disc two. He also reloaded the printer with a new half-ream of paper. When everything was set he looked at John and said. "Here we go. I've set the printer to make two copies of each page."

Both men sat down on Mike's office sofa and silently waited while the printer hummed for almost ten minutes. When the printer stopped, numerous pages had been printed for each copy set. Mike went over to the printer and grabbed the two stacks of printed sheets.

John said, "Look Mike, it's almost four o'clock

and it looks like we both have a lot to read. Let's both go home and secret ourselves away from our family and read what disc two is all about. I know we have to keep what we know ultra confidential. Even our wives have to be kept out of this for now. Why don't we meet in your office tomorrow at about 9:30 a.m. and discuss what we learned."

"John," Mike replied, "that's a very good plan. I frankly can't wait to get home and plow into this document. I am very nervous and excited at the same time. See you tomorrow at 9:30 a.m. sharp."

"Bye Mike" was John's reply as he walked out of Mike's office holding a thick sheaf of paper close to his chest as if he were protecting a personal treasure.

Disc Two

This journal will begin with a first entry date of April 28, 2011. I have been held by an unusual group of people for almost a week. They seem to mean us no harm but it is clear we are not allowed to leave where we are, so we can not return to our vehicles and venture back to the surface.

I plan to keep a journal or diary log of events here. I am doing this so I have something to refer back to as time goes by. I have a strange feeling that our group will be prohibited from returning to the surface for some time.

April 28, 2011

Today was like no other that I or the other five guys in our group ever experienced. When we arrived at the end of the tunnel, we saw that the "end point" had a very unusual closure. We were not sure what to do at that moment so we proceeded with something that did seem rather dumb. We started banging on the closure area with wrenches. At first this seemed so pointless. However, after about two minutes of this clanging we were amazed to find out that the closure area was actually a circular door mechanism that opened from the center in a spiral motion.

It took almost twenty minutes for the door to open fully. The area on the other side of the door had background lighting from some source so we could begin to peer inside. Gradually as the door aperture became larger, until the door was fully opened, light began to filter into our side of the tunnel so our flashlights could be turned off.

We were in a state of shock because on the other side of the circular doorway were the shapes of four beings. They were human in general form but also different and quite ominous. They remained stationary and did not come into our side of the tunnel. They stood as a group about fifty feet back from the tunnel door. All the time the door was opening they just stood there presumably looking at us.

All four of these beings were very tall. Each was the same height as the others and I would guess about seven feet tall. They were clothed with a shiny silver-blue covering much like a space suit except it looked more like shiny foil wrapping paper. Their suits covered everything but their heads. Their hands and feet were also covered with this same shiny material. Each wore a head piece. At least we thought it looked like a head piece. These head pieces or helmet gear were about eighteen inches long and had an oval top. The head pieces looked like tinted glass - the kind of glass you see in some limousines that allow you to see outside, but from the outside you are not able to see inside.

We carefully crossed the threshold to their side of the doorway. As we walked closer to them, they still stood motionless on their side of the tunnel. It was unnerving to move closer to them and yet they remained like inert statues.

All of a sudden, the one on the far left took a small step closer to us and moved his right arm in what we would call a universal motion for us to come forward toward them. We now looked at each other not sure how we should respond. I remember Angel saying "I'm not sure this is a good idea. They look pretty menacing." At that point Joe Smith answered.

"Look, if they meant us harm, we're dead meat anyway. What could we do to escape, start running twenty eight hundred miles through a dark tunnel? We are in this for better or for worse. I'm going!"

At that moment Joe started forward with the other five of us timidly starting to follow. I knew I would go also, but decided to quick run back to my electric cart cab and get my portable computer. I somehow hoped it might help in some way. It was just an instinctive reaction without a lot of fore-thought. The group stopped for about a minute so I had time to come back and join them again. When I returned, our group of five were only about fifteen feet away from these very tall creatures.

With arm and hand gestures they beckoned us to follow them as they turned and walked to their left. We were all petrified as to what would become of us. We figured we had little choice but to follow their lead because there would be no possible escape for us otherwise. As we walked farther away from the tunnel door opening, we looked back and saw the tunnel aperture door mechanism silently close behind us. I personally don't think I have ever been more frightened in my life. I felt weak-kneed and I know my hands were starting to quiver.

As they moved left, they began walking around what looked like a huge wall behind them. The top of the wall seemed to go sky high and stretched to infinity. As we all kept walking, one of them kept motioning with his arm for us to follow.

We were never so scared or nervous in our lives. None of us said a word. You could tell that we were all scared to death of what we might be facing. After a ten minute walk which probably covered about two thousand feet the group ahead of us came to a stop. One of them put his hand against a panel on the building. Immediately a doorway opened revealing an eight foot wide opening which was twelve feet high. The beings ahead of us walked into a large all white interior square chamber that looked about twenty five feet by twenty five feet. We slowly followed. After, Arnie who was last in our group, entered the room, the door behind us closed quickly. It was now the six of us and the four of them.

One of the four, not the one with the arm signals, came over to us and touched my clothing. He kept touching the buttons on my shirt and then pointing to a large plastic looking box at the side of the room. There were several such boxes all together. I just didn't get it. He kept touching my shirt buttons and point to the box. All of us were mystified. After about five minutes of this shirt-button nonsense, the being touching me, carefully unbuttoned two buttons and then pointed back to one of the boxes.

Niles said, "Ike, he wants you to take

your shirt off and put it in the box."

I felt like an idiot, but undid the remaining buttons and took off my shirt and put it in the box. Then the being went over to Steve and touched his shirt buttons and pointed. Pretty soon we all got the message and pulled our shirts off and put them in different boxes, one box for each of us.

With all of our shirts off, the being came over and touched our belts and pants pockets and again pointed to the boxes. Well, we pretty much guessed they wanted us to further undress. The drill went further over the next ten minutes with shoes, sox, watches, rings etc all going into the box. We all felt pretty vulnerable standing there in our underwear. We didn't know whether to feel foolish or frightened at this point. We do know we felt very vulnerable and that feeling was shared by all of us. They also took my portable computer and put it with my shed clothing.

The beings in front of us now pointed to our underwear and then to the box. They wanted us stripped down naked. I began to feel like we entered "The Land of the Perverts." What could we do at this point but to comply. There we were, six men standing naked in a room with four tall stronger beings.

After, we stood naked for about a minute, one of the beings put their hand to a side panel that opened a door which was half the size of the last door. They walked into another adjacent similar sized room. We followed, but before we could enter the next room, one of the beings held up his hand to stop us. We stopped. Then the door closed leaving our naked party of six alone in the first room.

We will never forget what occurred next. The room took on a green glow. Then our bodies were subjected to an experience unlike any we could ever have witnessed or contemplated. You know how your foot can fall asleep and later when you move it again, the blood starts to circulate again with a powerful tingling sensation. Imagine that tingling sensation over your whole body. Your ears, toes, arms, butt, neck - - - everything tingled. It wasn't painful but it was very uncomfortable. It went on for at least thirty minutes. Near the end Dr. Diamond - Niles, said "I think we are being cleansed of impurities that exist in our bodies. That would be my guess."

Later we would find out he was absolutely correct. Finally the procedure ended and the door to the other room opened. We were waved in to the next room. Angel tried to grab his box of clothes, but it became clear to him that the boxes were to be left behind when one of the beings took the box away from him and put it back with the other boxes.

Once in the next room we were in for the shock of our lives. The beings pulled off their suits and what we now know was a helmet and placed the items by a side wall.

They then stood there. The elongated helmet made them appear taller than they were. They were still tall, about six foot four each. They were very human except their skull shape was slightly elongated compared to us. I would say the distance from chin to top of head was on average three inches greater than what you would expect from a normal human skull.

We were facing three men and one woman. The men had short cropped blond hair on their heads. The woman also with blond hair, had small breasts evident. Her blonde hair was longer than her male friends, but still cropped relatively short by standards of most women who are humans on the surface. The stature of all four of these beings was very erect and tall. They were all similar to each other in facial structure. It was like seeing almost, but not quite, identical twins together. The woman was very beautiful in form and body structure, if you can get beyond the elongated head.

At this point they started talking to one another in an incomprehensible language. To me it sounded like a lot of k's, sh's, and nik's. In a sentence it would sound like "clap, nik, din, von, slik, klin, klasto, etc." It was very weird but they understood each other. As they talked, they remained expressionless, neither smiling or frowning.

After having what appeared to be a short discussion, they proceeded to undress until they were naked like us. It was really strange being all naked in this room together especially with a woman present. They actually looked like perfect physical specimens. Each was toned and solid without any trace of extra weight. The woman was a statuesque beauty. However, to slightly daunt her attractiveness, was again getting used to her elongated head.

When they finished undressing, a wall panel button was pressed and the room filled with a glowing golden-yellow light. Again, the tingling, but this time it was very light and honestly somewhat refreshing. Niles said to us, "Unless I am mistaken, we are taking a 'gang' shower together."

This experience only lasted about thirty seconds. After that, we followed them to still another adjacent room. In this room there were many shelf units along one wall. We were directed one at a time to a shelf until that held a silver-blue jumpsuit and attached plastic-like boots. There was not any underclothing. The beings themselves did not wear any underclothing when they dressed into their own silver-blue jumpsuits. Each of their jumpsuit tops had symbols across an area where a breast pocket would be on any ordinary shirt. These symbols were indecipherable to us. The writing was slightly different for each of the four beings. We presumed the symbols were an identifying name tag.

As we donned our new garments that were a bright and shiny silver-blue color, we felt like the material was a thin aluminum foil. However, they were surprisingly comfortable once put on to wear. They were complete form-fitting jumpsuits that required you to step into from an open middle section. The plastic like boots or shoes were attached to the pant legs. All our suits and theirs had a large zipper around the waist and down the crotch area for obvious functions.

After dressing, these beings ventured forward motioning us to follow them. Another button in a wall panel was pressed which opened a fairly large doorway. We walked through this doorway following our four guides. On the other side of this doorway we saw that we had entered a city. It looked vast. There was a blue sky or so it seemed. The height of the sky or painted sky, if that was the case, must have been at least two thousand feet high.

It was odd; but there were no noises or even people that were visible. The buildings ahead were mostly one or two stories. I saw a three story building a distance away. The streets seemed like a hard light tan plastic surface. What was really unusual was that no one cast a shadow. The filtered light from above was evidently so evenly disbursed that any shadows could not exist. The temperature was very comfortable, not warm or too cool.

Our fear, or at least mine, was starting to ebb. Although still wary, I was now quite curious as to what was in store for our group.

We were escorted out into what seemed to be a street. As far as we could see were one and two story vanilla colored buildings with brown doors. Every one hundred feet or so was another door. There were not any shops and we still did not see anyone else on the street we entered. As a group of ten (four of them and six of us) we walked slowly down the street. We followed our guides. They seldom looked back at us probably feeling very self-assured that we would stay close behind them.

Every five or six hundred yards we would come to an intersection. As we looked sideways into another street we continued to see a very long street which looked identical to the one we were currently walking along.

After perhaps a mile or so, we were joined by two other beings who looked almost identical in size and stature to the four beings who were ahead of us. As they met, they talked to each other for a few minutes. Shortly after, they split into three teams of two. The one woman and a man came over to Joe Smith and I and indicated we should follow them. This was repeated with each team of two beings dividing the rest of our group. After our group of six was divided, we started to walk in separate groups of four - - two beings and two of us.

We walked for about another one half mile with our two leaders and ourselves staying close behind. We looked back and saw that the other two groups of four were not to be seen, probably having made a turn into the last intersection we passed.

Our two leaders stopped by one of the brown doors which had symbols on the door which matched the identifying symbols on their clothing. Joe and I talked to each other surmising they were entering their designated home. They opened the door which was obviously left unlocked. As we entered the home we came into a very large room about thirty feet by thirty feet square. A light came on immediately. Actually it wasn't a light so much as the entire ceiling area illuminated itself so that we were bathed in a white-yellow ambient light.

As we looked around, Joe and I commented to each other on the very spartan furnishings. There was a table about twice the size of an ordinary card table with four chairs. The chairs were translucent and appeared very basic in structure which was the same as the table. There was no other furniture in the room. There were four cut outs in the walls. Each was three feet in depth, four feet in height and eight feet in length. Each cut out was about two feet above the floor. In each cut out area was a white mat about three inches thick. Joe and I quickly came to the conclusion that these were beds for sleeping.

We saw a brown door at one end of the room. We took it upon ourselves to go over and open that door without asking. Inside we were surprised to see a somewhat conventional bathroom. There was a toilet much like we would expect to see except it was about three inches higher off the ground than a conventional toilet. This higher toilet was obviously designed for the height of the occupants. There was a shower stall next to the toilet. There was no evidence of any water spray nozzle which seemed very curious.

Also in the bathroom was a small cut-out in the wall that was about eighteen inches by eighteen inches and about twelve inches deep. This cut out was about five feet off the floor. This cut-out area was totally empty.

We left the bathroom area and went over across the room to another area which was cut out of the wall. This cut out area was six feet tall rising directly from the floor. It was about three feet wide and three feet deep. A single clear plastic pole was evident with four plastic looking hangers.

Other than what I have described, the room was empty. The floor was a hard white plastic-like surface.

After our hosts let us explore and talk, they came over and pointed for us to be seated at the table. After we were seated, they touched a button on the wall which allowed for a section of the wall to open.

In the opening was a dispenser of sorts and various bowls and spoons. The man host took a bowl and placed it under the dispenser and pushed a small lever. A thick flowing substance poured out into a bowl. The bowl was brought over to me with a spoon. This was repeated for Joe who sat beside me. The male and female host did the same for themselves and then sat at the table with us.

Our two hosts did not talk to each other but began to eat the porridge looking meal in front of them. Obviously we were supposed to dine on this goo or go hungry. We lifted our spoons and cautiously took a small portion and put it in our mouths. This porridge looked like oatmeal. It had the taste of a mixture of vanilla pudding, applesauce and spinach. It didn't taste bad but at the same time was a far cry from any epicurean delight. Although Joe and I talked, our two hosts were silent much like a married couple who had been together too long and had nothing to say to each other. They were oblivious to any conversation between Joe and I.

Our hosts finished first and sat by quietly until we were done. After we finished they took our bowls and spoons back to the dispenser area and pressed a button. There was a noise and a bright blue light. I went over to see what was going on only to discover that our bowls and spoons were now completely clean.

Our male host reached deep into the opening and pulled out small plastic tumblers which he proceeded to fill from an adjacent dispenser which we failed to notice at first. A light orange liquid was put into each of four tumblers and brought over to the table. Our host unceremoniously drank the liquid quickly. Joe and I followed suit but much more cautiously. The liquid drink tasted like lightly flavored water. It was refreshing.

Again after we all finished our drink, the glasses were taken back to the dispenser and shoved to the rear. The button was again pushed to activate the ray or whatever it was that cleansed the bowls and spoons a few moments ago.

Abruptly, the woman came over and pointed or gestured that we should remove our jumpsuit garment which would leave us naked. She took off her garment leaving her fully exposed as we were. The male host did the same. Our garments were placed on hangers in the closet. Another button was pushed and a light blue glow emanated from the closet.

After the garments were hung up, the man and the woman placed themselves into their designated bed cut-outs. They gestured for us to do the same. Evidently sleeping in this strange civilization was a procedure accomplished without any nightwear.

Within a few minutes of placing ourselves in the bed cut-out, I fell asleep. Next morning Joe reiterated the same experience. Frankly, this was the most pleasant complete sleep experience I ever had. It was a sound restful uninterrupted sleep that left me refreshed and invigorated when I awoke the next morning.

April 29, 2011

Our awakening the next morning was due to hearing our two hosts move about the room. They were already dressed in their jumpsuit garments. As soon as they saw Joe and I wake, they gestured we follow them to the bathroom area. Once inside they had both Joe and I take turns entering the shower stall. There was not any soap or water evident. Our host pushed a button reaching inside the shower enclosure and a light golden-yellow colored light came on very similar to the second cleansing shower we witnessed yesterday.

Again we felt the mild tingling sensation and after about twenty seconds of that, our host reached into the shower to shut down the light beams. We were motioned at that point to leave the shower area and go to the closet and retrieve our clothing. Our clothes were fresh and clean. I noticed a spot on the boot yesterday that was no longer evident. It would appear we will probably wear the same clothing day after day.

After dressing myself, I saw my computer sitting on the one table in the room. During the night someone must have brought it to me. I went over to examine the portable computer and proceeded to boot it up. The computer came on and the indicator showed full battery power available. On the side of the computer where a charger could be plugged in, was a three inch long cylinder now permanently attached to the computer. Obviously I was the beneficiary of a power source so that I could use my device. I was also given four diskettes that were placed on the table beside my computer. These beings had evidently studied this equipment overnight and created a power source adapter and disks for my use.

The first thing I did before our breakfast was to journal what happened yesterday which brings you up to speed with where we are now. In fact, one of our hosts has motioned for me to put my computer on my bed area so the table can be used for a morning meal.

April 29, 2011

I am writing this entry after dinner and before bed. Our two hosts have tucked themselves in along with Joe and are sleeping soundly. Our hosts seem not to be troubled with my staying up with my computer. I guess this will start a routine on my part of recording what has occurred here.

I will start with today following breakfast which consisted of the same meal and drink as last night. And we had the same meal again tonight. This seems to be the only food available from the spigot used to fill our dinner bowls.

We left our residence unit right after breakfast. No one brushed their teeth. We do clean our hands in the bathroom by inserting them in the eighteen by eighteen cut out which I first saw yesterday. The light golden-yellow light comes on and our hands are cleaned just like our bodies were when we entered the shower stall.

We walked as a group of four down our street and made a right turn up a new street after about two hundred yards of travel. Within about a hundred feet after making the right turn we stopped at a bright blue door which our hosts opened for all of us to enter.

Upon entering, we found ourselves in a

narrow hallway with stairs going downward. The stairwell was brightly lit from the ceiling. I counted about fifty steps before we reached a landing directly in front of an area that could only be an elevator.

Our hosts pushed a button which brought the elevator to our level. We entered the elevator which was a basic stark affair with six vertical buttons. The fourth button from the top was pressed. The elevator responded. Within about ten seconds we were at the designated floor. The elevator opened and we followed our hosts out.

After walking a few paces into a larger area we stoped in front of a wall with what was obviously a doorway. Shortly the doorway opened automatically and a subway travel car was in front of us to enter. We followed our hosts inside and took seats. There were two other passengers already in the vehicle.

The vehicle shot out of there with great speed as soon as the vehicle door shut. We only traveled for about twenty seconds, but I had the sensation of great acceleration. Joe also experienced the same feeling himself.

When we stopped and followed our hosts out, we found ourselves in a vast underground plaza. It seems funny to make a further underground distinction since this whole civilization exists in an underground environment. We looked around and saw dozens of men and women moving from place to place. All of the men and women had very similar features to our two host guides. Everyone wore the same shiny jumpsuits. The only distinguishing item was the lettering or symbols that appeared on the breast portion of their garment. We saw very little communication between these people. They all seemed to have a mission.

We walked about two hundred yards across the plaza area and were ushered into a small building. Once in the building, Joe and I were separated. The female host took me to a chamber room where three other beings, all males, were waiting.

I was motioned to sit in a chair facing a large monitor screen. Two one inch round disks were put on my temple areas held loosely by a hook that fit over my ears. It was not uncomfortable to have these items touching my temple area.

One of the new beings we just met, stood in front of me and pointed to his eye. He kept touching his eye until I said the word eye.

Once I uttered that word, the screen came to life with a picture of an eye, the spelling of eye in English from my memory, and the phonetic sound for an eye with my exact mid western accent.

After eye, the leader in front of me went through all the body parts with my repeating what he pointed at with his finger. Each time the screen lit up with symbol, sound, and spelling responses from my mind.

We spent countless hours going over body parts. After the body parts they showed objects of pictures to me such as tables, chairs, clothing etc. After a while I was encouraged to think out loud with naming objects that came to mind. Each time I thought of an item like a towel, a shovel, a car, or an emotion, it played out in pictures, sounds and a written spelling. I was exhausted when we finished for the day.

As we left this sort of an interrogation facility, Joe and I met up again. He had the exact same experience. We both assumed that our other four companions, Steve, Arnie, Niles, and Angel probably were treated similarly.

It is now after dinner, and I am recording this entry with my last ounce of strength. I am just dog tired!

May 8, 2011

I am writing this after having completed a tenth straight day of this unusually mental image interrogation process. Joe has had the same experience for each day and we compare notes when the day is over and we are having dinner.

Today's inquiry or probing our minds procedure ended early. We were taken back to our normal residential quarters earlier than usual. Our two hosts sat by and watched Joe and I converse. They did not seem to communicate to each other. Later, dinner and bedtime was as per usual.

As we placed ourselves in our respective sleep booths, surprisingly the female host spoke for the first time to us. Her words were in a crisp clear yet unemotional tone. "Good night. Have a good sleep."

May 9, 2011

Today started out quite differently than the past ten days. When we left our residence unit, we were soon joined by our four other comrades who we had not seen for some time. As we walked, we were a grouping of the six of us and our six hosts who walked beside us in silence.

When we first saw each other that morning, we hugged and smiled being reassured that no harm had come to any in our group. As we walked, we talked and shared experiences. It seems that the interrogation treatment for Joe and I was identical to what everyone else in our group had to endure.

After a fairly long walk we entered a building and were ushered into a small auditorium of sorts. The six of our group were motioned to sit in front chairs while our hosts were quietly seated behind us. Two different beings stood in front of us.

After we were settled in, one of the two beings, who were new to us, moved directly in front of us and spoke to us in clear unaccented English. His address was along the lines of what I will recite now as I remember it being so fresh in my mind.

"Gentleman, First of all we welcome your visit. I am sure you are wondering what the past days have been all about. Through our mental probing technology and your excellent cooperation, we learned the basic language of your above-ground civilization. At this point only myself and my colleague (the being pointed to the other person standing beside him) have been fully versed in communicating with you fully understanding your language. Your host guides that you live with are partially versed in your language."

"For the next few days, you will be asked to write down why you have come here and what do you expect of us. We need to understand your objectives in order to prepare to handle your visit properly. We also expect that you will write out your personal biographies so we know the background and history for each of you. While you perform these tasks, your normal residential hosts will spend more time learning your language. They have only so far learned a few words. We are also going to share your language with other key individuals so that as you tour around and spend more time with us, questions can be answered for you."

"We knew of your impending visit from the moment you opened the door way to the tunnel many days ago. We have monitored your journey progress continually. This is the first time we have ever been visited by individuals who live on the surface of the planet. We have concerns and apprehensions as to what the knowledge of our civilization existing will have upon us if your world has awareness of our presence."

As quickly as he finished, we were walked to another room where each of us was seated at a small desk. In front of us was paper and a writing instrument much like a pencil. The document in front of us was many pages with innumerable questions to answer. We all discovered an astounding thing. If we made a mistake and wrote something we wished to change, all we had to do is wand the pencil-like point over the item to be corrected and the wrong entry would disappear.

There were many sections where we were to write our own histories in our own words, going beyond just responding to questions.

This process took all of today and we were far from complete at the end of the day. I can only guess that we will be back at it tomorrow.

When we finished, our normal hosts joined us as we took the long walk back to our residential units.

As was usually the case, we ate the same meal and were put to bed at the same time as our hosts. Our hosts were again silent tonight despite supposedly having another day of English language immersion.

May 11, 2011

We finished a third day of answering questions and writing about ourselves. As we finished to leave for our long walk home, our female host said very clearly "Please follow us back. We are all tired from a long day. Tomorrow will be very different for you."

That was it, but a real breakthrough to finally break the "sound barrier" with these two beings who we have been living with for two weeks.

It was amusing to me, that they entered their sleep cut-outs knowing I was up alone with my computer, as usual. This time I said "good night" and I was shocked to get a response back of "Good night Ike."

Before I quit, I need to mention that every night my computer remains at full power. It would seem the power source attachment permanently placed on my computer is somewhat an inexhaustible source of energy.

May 12, 2011

Today was an absolute revelation for me and I think I could speak for all six of us. Our morning started as usual with getting up, cleansing, dressing and breakfast. The only difference this morning, came just prior to our dressing. Our male host asked very matter-of-factly "why we had hair on various parts of our body in addition to the hair on our heads."

I was somewhat taken aback with the abruptness of the question. My answer went something to the order of "we call ourselves human beings and it is in our genetic make-up to grow hair on parts of our body. Some beings have more hair than others. We are an evolving species. I think some of our ancestors thousands of years ago had much more hair than we do now." I had thought about going into the theory of evolving from hairy apes, but realized this could only serve to get into an area of knowledge where I felt ill-equipped to make a lot of sense. My explanation seemed to satisfy the question because there was no follow up interest in this subject.

Before Joe and I left, Joe approached both of our hosts with an overture of introduction. "Let's introduce ourselves, my name is Joe Smith and (pointing to me) my friend's name is Ike Tenner. We would like to know names on how to address you."

Our two hosts looked at each other and had a brief interchange in their language before moving closer to us. The male answered as follows. "You may call me Denar and my female companion is called Rekak. We already knew your names."

At that point it got humorous. Joe put his hand out in front of him to shake hands with Denar. Denar put his hand in front of him, but clearly did not understand the gesture of shaking one's hand. Joe started to laugh and so did I. Our laughter caught both Denar and Rekak off guard until Joe explained the handshake meeting gesture. He took Denar's hand and shook it gently. Denar shook his hand but didn't know when to let go. Denar was very strong and it took some effort for Joe to extract his hand. When he got his hand free, he covered the handshake gesture more completely and Joe tried it again. This time Denar responded well and Rekak came over to try the same thing with me. I don't think they understood our amusement at the farcical event of a few moments ago. Both Joe and I felt that spontaneous humor was lacking with these two and perhaps everyone we met since we never saw any individual smile since we arrived.

Soon we were out the door where our group of four was joined by Steve, Arnie, Niles and Angel plus their hosts. We were taken to the same small auditorium as yesterday. Again we were seated in front with our hosts behind us.

A new person from this civilization stood in front of us and began to speak after he had the attention of everyone.

"My name is Jonar. I have ultimate responsibility for your visiting us. I officially welcome you, but I say that with some deep apprehension. Over the past days we have learned your language. Many of your word responses and projected images were found quite troubling. (At this point Jonar pulled a long list from a pocket in his clothing.) Words like attack, kill, self defense, war, hit, murder, deceive, trickery, yell, anger, theft, mischief, hide, betray, plus about a hundred similar words seem to convey a culture where people are unkind or malicious to a fellow individual. We have never witnessed any behaviors like this in our civilization. We want to know if this is how you regularly act or is there some explanation that can comfort us?

At that point Niles Diamond stood up and spoke for us. "First of all I can assure you we come to you peacefully with no harmful intention. The words you chose from our vocabulary represent our knowledge of poor behaviors for a small minority of individuals who live on the surface of the planet. Most all people on earth, our name for this planet, are hard working, responsible and trustworthy people. Our vocabulary and knowledge of the worst people on our planet should only be taken as general knowledge and not a reflection of any of us or our intentions. We are your guests and we come in a good cause - to know about you."

Jonar looked at us carefully and responded "I will take you at your stated peaceful intention. There is another word that is used commonly by all of you and yet it represents a paradox to us. In our civilization we respect each other with every individual being an equal. Each of us contributes in their own special way. Words like love, adore, kindness, and other words seem to exist in your civilization while at the same time you convey words of interaction with each other such as mistrust, adultery, condescending, dislike plus others. We do not understand."

Joe Smith stood up this time. "The fact that you are perplexed with the incongruity of our behavior is justified. Even though we as a species mean well towards each other, we are emotional individuals. We can have happy moments and sad moments. We can one day like another individual and at another time despise this same person. We are complex. All I can say is that the six of us want to visit with you, earn your trust and learn about you. From many things we have seen in our short time, you have made advances in technology and civilized practices that we envy and want very much to better understand."

Jonar walked over to the three men and one woman who were standing off to one side. "These individuals will be your tour guides. Wherever you go, they will lead and provide information and learning. Wherever you go, your residential hosts will also be with you."

Jonar continued. "Before we begin I will give each of you paper and a writing instrument. I want all six of you to put down on that paper five questions about us or items of interest you wish to learn more about. From this list we will create a logical touring program starting tomorrow. Today, after this meeting, we will take you around our city by walking or subway. This will be a general tour."

After we finished our list of five items, we were gathered as a group to tour a sampling of areas in this seemingly vast city. The first stop was I suppose the City Utilities which explained how they exist underground.

After two short subway rides we were in an area with one extremely large building in front of us. We were told that it was a power plant. Soon we discovered this was a nerve center which was much much more than a single place where power was created.

The building in front of us was the size of about three large football stadiums, side by side. I would guess the height to the roofline at about one hundred feet. We were not allowed inside. Electricity, or a form of it was the power output. It was explained that the power source was the harnessing and enhancement of magnetic energy and the management of pole reversals. Joe Smith sort of began to understand, but the rest of us just listened.

We were told that thousands of power lines were placed underground that supplied electricity to all parts of the city. This building also contained an air filtration plant that took in air from all parts of the city and refreshed that air continually.

We were next walked to a small factory-looking building about one-half mile from the power plant. In this building we were led inside. The primary purpose for this building was the creation of the shiny material used for everyone's clothing. We saw evidence of a process where liquid chemicals were mixed. Later that mixture went through a chamber where the liquid flowed to a flat surface steel plate. The plate now having a thin coating of liquid went through intense heat and later freezing environments. At the end, a continuous run of the shiny silvery blue fabric spewed out of a machine. We were informed that this fabric was taken to another area of the city where it was stretched and eventually cut to become the clothing we were wearing.

May 15, 2011

Today was our fourth day of general touring. We were shown how the city was fed. We were guided to the area where the liquid we drink is created. It essentially is distilled water which is later infused with concentrated minerals and vitamins required by all life forms.

The entire day was spent on the production of food. We were taken to what could best be called a farm at the outer reaches of the city. This farm was vast. I would guess it was at least a mile square. We saw many vegetables we recognized plus several we learned about that we had never seen before. Everything is grown hydroponically. Nothing is grown in soil.

The time period from the bud of a vegetable to full growth is measured in days. The eventual size of the harvested vegetable is enormous compared to what we expected. We saw three foot long carrots and tomatoes the size of basketballs.

The harvested vegetables are taken to an area where measured amounts of each vegetable are pulverized into a paste. Special nutrients are added to this mixture with again concentrated vitamins. Enough water is added to form a slurry which flows. This mixture is then forced through a piping system to all residential areas. We tasted the flowing goo and sure enough, it was the same stuff we eat every morning and every night. As I might have said before it gets a "four" on the scale of one is awful and ten is delicious. They say hunger is the best sauce and that's what makes us look forward to whatever we are fed. I must say however, for the weeks we have been here, no one has had an upset stomach or any digestive problems whatsoever.

We are all vegetarians now. There are no animals or fowl in existence in this civilization. We are told there is a small pond where fish are raised to create part of the nutrient and vitamin mix which is added to the food.

With no animals, the idea of having a pet is unknown here. We talked about that concept to our hosts and they were incredulous with the idea that we would keep animals around once we explained what animals were like and which ones made good pets and which did not. They were bewildered as to why anyone would be around a pet animal that no one could have any communication on any intellectual level. The more we told them about pets and that we eat some animals, the more our hosts looked at us like unkempt barbarians.

As I write this entry, I must say I am looking forward to tomorrow. We are told it will be explained why all these people look similar and what their lives are like for the average individual.

May 16, 2011

We were first taken today for an explanation and an overview as to how these people are born and why they look so very much alike. This was a lecture really.

The woman leading the lecture talked about the sperm and egg concept. There are no pregnancies here for gestation. When a new life form is required, a select male and female are chosen where their sperm contribution and egg contribution are taken and put together in a controlled environment. The fetus process is a procedure of ten and one half months, not the nine that are the case with our human race.

The two donors go away after their respective contribution. There is no concept of parenthood or attachment to the growing fetus or the later birthed child.

At any one year there are fifty fetuses in various stages of growth. Boys and girls are always created on an equal basis. We were told the population of this city is fifteen thousand individuals. There are exactly seventy-five hundred males and seventy five hundred females.

During the fetus process and early childhood stages of development, there is a strict regimen of genetic monitorization. Every individual birth is fully known by a mapped out genetic matrix that was pre planned. The study of genetics has been a field of complete understanding for tens of thousands of years.

Every birthed individual has a predetermined place in society. Some have a genetic disposition to clean, to organize, to build, to create, to lead others, to doctor, to farm, to repair and perform maintenance, to work on assembly lines in manufacturing, to be plumbers, etc, etc, etc. This genetic dispositioning allows each person to love their particular job and never have any envy of anyone else's role in life. People here look forward to every day they do their jobs. Everyone is genetically ordered so the concept of "dissatisfaction" does not exist. Everyone here is an equal. A leader is no better a person and is not on any higher standing than one who cleans or farms or any other line of work.

There is no concept here of wages, money, wealth or attainment. Each person loves his job, and expects to end each day at a residence where he or she can sleep and receive food. Also, I must say the concept of a day off does not exist here. To live, is to work and that is a joy and a purpose for every person.

An interesting question was posed by Niles Diamond. He asked them to explain how they can only birth fifty beings per year and still maintain their population level of fifteen thousand persons. The answer was shocking.

The average life span of each being in this city is about three hundred years. All those years are years of good physical and mental health.

Joe and I asked Denar and Rekak their ages. They didn't know and asked Jonar to answer the question. Jonar had a small hand held device, probably a computer which was taken out of his pocket. Jonar must have keyed in the question to some data bank. The answer came back within a minute. Jonar came over to us and stated that their records show Denar as 225 years old and Rekak as 110 years old. After hearing this, we glanced back at both of them. Until now, Joe and I would have judged them both to be in their early twenties. They were strong, muscular, had chiseled features, and not the slightest sign of a wrinkle, a liver spot, or any other sign of advancing age.

We were told that if a farm worker was needed to be born, then the sperm and egg donation would come from persons who do farm work.

Another question asked was why did they manage their genetic engineering so individuals were so much alike in height, muscular build, blond hair, blue eyes, and facial structure. The answer went to their concept of equalization. It was felt that persons of similar features would never be jealous of the physique or attractive countenance of another person.

Later in the day we were taken to a

fascinating futuristic laboratory where we were shown fetuses in clear plastic chambers of fluid. The growth points spanned from microscopic embryos to a child about to be removed from his/her life support nutrient system. We were amazed. There were twenty six girls and twenty five boys. The difference balanced off the loss of an aged woman earlier this month.

After that, we toured a school/work environment where the ages ranged from toddler to adolescent. It was explained that classroom education and work introduction went hand in hand in their life learning instructional process. We did not witness any playtime or recreational equipment available. Again as with adults, no one smiled and yet at the same time there was no evidence that any child was unhappy.

It was a very long day, but certainly an eye-opener for all of us. Joe and I sat at the dinner table and interchanged our observations and opinions. As we talked out loud, Denar and Rekak certainly overheard what we said but chose to remain silent. They seldom talked to each other and only to us when we directed a question their way.

May 31, 2011

We are with Denar and Rekak day and night. They are always cordial to us but never initiate any conversation with us. They will patiently answer our questions in excellent English when we direct an inquiry their way. Curiously they speak to each other in their special language only on seldom occasions. We do notice that there is some kind of telepathic bond which seems to always operate. If one of them plans to go move our table, the other is there to assist at the exact same moment. Bedtime is simultaneous for both of them even though there is no clock evident. When they do retire for the evening it usually ranges between 9:30 p.m. and 10:00 p.m. on our watches which were returned to us recently. Again, they will both undress for bed at the exact same second with no oral communication at all.

Over the past two evenings, just following our porridge supper, I directed some interesting questions to Denar and Rekak.

I asked whether they had any wonder or curiosity about what was occurring on the surface of the planet. Rekak gave an answer that seems to address the depth of genetic engineering which has occurred. She responded as follows: "No one thinks about the surface. We live here. Why should we think about the surface?"

I tried to engage conversation with Rekak. "Well for one thing your people once lived on the surface. For another, don't you wonder about what lives above you presently? Don't you have any interest in asking Joe or I what our surface lives were like compared to life here?"

I expected some retort but was taken aback with the complete lack of interest. Without meaning to be rude or unsociable, Rekak simply said "We don't think about the surface," walked to the other side of the room and spoke for a second out loud to Denar who just looked back at us and never spoke himself. Their complete lack of interest in most everything is a little unnerving.

I asked Rekak if she recognized some people in the city as friends versus other people who they did not know or had never met before. The answer again was difficult to fathom. She just said, "What are friends?"

I explained the concept versus strangers. She said everyone was her friend even if she never met them yet. Obviously there was a disconnect to get an answer like that. Liking someone more than another person seems to be a concept which does not exist.

Three nights ago I took out my computer and played a song which was in memory. Denar and Rekak listened without expression.

When the song was over they were asked if they liked to hear the music I played. With a placid countenance Rekak spoke for both of them. "The sounds seem pleasant to hear. Why do you play these sounds?"

I felt I might be starting a real conversation since I was actually asked a question. I responded about why people enjoy music because it sounds nice to the ear, it is often relaxing, it can make people feel good. Then she killed the conversation by just answering, "I understand." There just seems to be no interest in doing anything, learning more, or getting excited or passionate about anything.

I see by the time we will be going to bed soon. I am going to ask Denar if he has any fears like dying, fear of heights, getting injured, or doing a bad job in their workplace.

Well I asked the questions. They never think about dying so there is no fear. Why would you fear heights if you are standing on something was another response. He never responded to fear of injury at all. I did get a half-way comprehensive response on doing poor work. "If I do work which was not done well, someone will tell me my work needs to be better. That person will show me how to do better work. After that my work will be better?"

I feel sometimes I am living with simple children who have no capacity to inquire. I feel these people are innately quite intelligent but the need to explore or learn new things seems to have been bred right out of their race.

June 15, 2011

It has been fifteen days since my last journal entry in the computer. Often, the end of the day makes me a little too tired to write down what I have seen.

Over this time, we have seen classroom training for children and adults. Data field management and general computerization skills are refreshed regularly for everyone. We saw equipment being repaired. We saw evidence of a rare death which I shall cover later. We saw beings getting haircuts, which by the way now included us. Our hair is now cropped in much the same fashion as our hosts.

Of great interest was the fact that these beings have three underground cities, not just one. This is the main city. Two other ten thousand person cities are situated several hundred miles north and south of this main city. Subways link these cities to each other and the travel time is only about ten minutes. We were all allowed to see each of these other cities. It was amazing that we traveled north to one of the cities and covered the four hundred plus miles in twelve minutes. We calculated our subway car traveled at about two thousand miles per hour. Yet our ride was smooth and quiet. The technology at play here is so far beyond anything I have ever heard about.

The other two cities were created as a just in case measure to preserve the species in case an earthquake or some shift in rock strata might occur that would cause any given city to be devastated. The other two cities seemed just like our main city with buildings looking like what we were used to seeing. Every city is self sufficient in its own right. The people we saw in the other two cities were very much identical to the main city itself.

We spent a couple of weeks back in the interrogation auditorium where we talked about what we knew of the history of our earth. As usual, when we had a thought our minds translated what we were thinking to a picture which showed up on the screen in front of us. Our interrogating hosts were actually eager to learn what our lives were like on the surface of the planet. They were extremely interested to know we had developed rudimentary rocket travel that allowed humans to leave the boundaries of earth. The fact that we put people on the moon and had a rocket land on Mars was causing quite a stir with all of them. I think there is something here that we may find out more about at a later time.

July 8, 2011

I generally now only make data log notations on the computer when something noteworthy has occurred. Since my last entry we have been taken around the city to talk to a multitude of residents. In advance, each resident we spoke to was given a crash course in our language. I don't know how they do it, but they speak English fairly fluently after a three day immersion course.

We have been talking to individuals in all types of trades and work. These people are incredibly content with their regimented lives. The fulfillment that comes from doing their jobs is something to behold. Everyone is friendly and honest. When we laugh or smile, they are perplexed with our expression of emotion.

Sometimes we explain what their job is like on the surface of the planet. They seem interested but aloof at the same time. We are a curiosity, I'm sure, but we seldom get many questions. Gestures of handshakes, pats on the back, and smiles are received cautiously.

As time is going on, I saw something occurring with our group of six. Joe and I are like sponges always wanting to know more about this very strange subterranean civilization. On the other hand, I sense Steve,

Niles, Arnie and Angel are becoming less interested in these people and bonding more together as a clique.

July 12, 2011

Yesterday and today were days I will never forget. Yesterday was a normal day of going out and being introduced to still more residents. This time it was again farm workers.

At the end of the day, we returned back to our residence and had the usual dinner, which I now look forward to and believe it or not have a acquired a taste for the subtle flavors.

Anyway, as per usual, we took off our clothes to retire. Without really thinking, I found myself staring at the sleek and alluring body of Rekak. My interest in her was showing "up" as you can quickly imagine. It was obvious she noticed my arousal state. I don't know what she said to Denar, but I can bet it was about me.

I was more than embarrassed and quickly went to my sleeping berth turning to the inside facing the wall.

The next day an unusual turn of events occurred after our morning meal. Joe went with Rekak to join our group for the day. I was walked in a different direction being alone with Denar. Denar did not speak as I followed him down an elevator to a subway for a short ride to the far end of the city. I was more than curious what was going on because I had never been split up from Joe before. At last Denar and I found ourselves in front of a fairly large two story building. Denar turned around before entering and spoke to me. I couldn't believe at first what I was being told.

He mentioned that Rekak was quite aware of my male arousal state the night before. Denar said our language provided reference to what he phrased as a build-up of sexual tension. Denar without so much as a blush or smile said this is not at all uncommon for the men and women in their civilization.

The building I would be entering alone was a way of being matched with women who were entering the building today to satisfy their heightened sexual requirements.

Denar said that I would enter the building and join a line of men in front of me. When I would finally get to the front of the line I would be escorted to a room where a woman would enter for her needs of gratification. In this room we would be allowed as much time as we wished to take.

Denar gave me a few cautions. I could certainly speak to the woman, but it would be unlikely that she would be among the few women so far selected in the city to learn English. She may answer in her language or not, but most certainly would not understand what I am saying anymore than I would make sense of her spoken words. Denar said touching, caressing and any manner of contact is acceptable. However, Denar explained that he had learned that our language had the word kiss where lips of two beings met together. He stated strongly, "do not kiss the woman." This act would likely be viewed offensively for lack of understanding on her part. Hugging was apparently okay, but kissing was definitely not going to be tolerated.

After the brief guidance from Denar, I entered the building with the dual feelings of trepidation and sexual excitement at the same time. There were many men ahead of me and I stood in line for at least an hour. The men in front of me and behind me paid no attention to me whatsoever. These men did not even speak to each other. It was strange to be in a long line of men where silence was the order of the day.

I was finally at the front of the line where an escort took me up some stairs to a long hallway. It looked like the long hallway of a cheap hotel. The plastic floors and smooth walls were immaculate but also cold lacking any decor. The hallway was well lit and I could see about twenty doors on each side of the hall. Each door had a marking which I assumed was a number.

My escort seemed oblivious to the fact that I was a shorter and a different structured male than everyone else. I was treated the same as every other man in line. Ahead I could see some men in the distance coming out of some of the doorways.

Out of a doorway about forty feet away, a woman came out and told the escort that the room was ready. I followed her to the doorway left open and was gestured by her to enter. After I was inside, she remained in the hallway and closed the door behind me. I was alone in a well lit room with a padded five inch mattress on the floor covered with a shiny light green sheet. As I looked around the room I saw two shower compartments and wall hooks for our clothing. Across the room was another door entrance just like the one I entered. Evidently women enter the building from a different hallway and doorway.

I was alone in this room for about two minutes when finally the door opened and a young beautiful female entered. She wore a shiny jumpsuit like mine. In fact she looked very much like Rekak, but perhaps an inch shorter in height.

For about a minute we just visually took each other in without a word or smile. She proceeded to slip out of her clothing and of course I was quick to follow. After we put our clothing on the wall hooks we cautiously walked to the center of the room being now only about four feet apart. I think she knew right away I was probably one of the aliens from the planet's surface. This fact was now well known by everyone. She stared at the hair under my arms, my chest hair, and pubic hairs.

She came closer and very gently touched

the hair on my chest, checking out the novelty. To me her touch was enticing. She was an exquisite beauty from the neck down. Her somewhat elongated head (like Rekak) still seemed strange, but I felt myself about to emotionally seize the moment and overlook her facial structure difference.

As she touched me, I felt that in good conscience I could follow her lead and gently caress her very sleek and toned body. Both of us were getting turned on fairy quickly.

I am not one for writing about this encounter going into explicit erotic details. I feel we both responded to each other mutually. It was a pleasurable and amazing encounter. We probably spent about twenty-five minutes all together with each other.

At the end, we both got on our feet. I smiled at her. She did not smile, but I could honestly sense an inner pleasure for what we shared. We quickly dressed. She nodded her head at me before exiting the room and I returned the gesture. After leaving the room, I was escorted out of the building where Denar stood calmly waiting for me.

Denar made no comment and only stated to follow him in order to join the rest of our group for the remainder of the day.

After dinner, I explained my experience to Joe who of course wondered why I went with Denar elsewhere. He was fascinated with my explaining what happened. He said he would probably make a suggestion to Denar in the morning, for himself to have the same experience I enjoyed. After stating that plan, we both laughed and went directly to our beds.

July 29, 2011

Our daily routine of touring continues. Each day Joe and I are met by Arnie, Angel, Steve and Niles. Whenever there are the six of us together, we are either touring or in a lecture room getting briefed on the culture that exists here. The six of us are never alone.

Now more than ever, I sense that the other four men of our group are getting anxious about being here for so long. I sense a certain separation in spirit from Joe and I. I don't fully know what to make of this phenomenon, but it has made me a little concerned.

August 6, 2011

As time was going by, our daily touring was designed to answer the questions we posed about two months ago. Today's tour dealt with illness, injury and death.

First we were taken to a hospital building. It was surprisingly a very small hospital with only about ten beds, an operating room, and a lobby. A doctor came to greet us when we entered. He received his crash course in English a few days ago in anticipation of this meeting with the six of us.

He stated that through genetic controls, diseases were almost unknown. The most common injury was a fall where a sprain or a broken limb or hip was experienced. There were two patients in the hospital now. One had broken an arm yesterday and the other slipped on some stairs and broke their hip.

He showed us the operating room. In most cases an operation is designed to align a broken bone or provide a filler replacement for a shattered hip or bones. The doctor pointed to a tube with a light fixture on the end that is lowered and applied to the treated area. The purpose is to accelerate cell growth and heal time. In most cases simple fractures are repaired and healed in three days. Hips and shattered bones take seven days. At the end of those periods, the patients walk out fully recovered.

Once in a great while a rare disease, or a birth defect is encountered. This is treated with tissue implantation and genetic reordering. This is a longer process taking up to thirty days before full health is restored.

The only fatal injuries are head injuries. The difference between life and death is one of discovery and being taken to the hospital in time. Most head injuries are treated on time, but once in a while, a patient arrives too late and the brain has been deprived of oxygen for too long a period. When recovery is not possible, the unconscious patient is not treated but rather put through a procedure where a quick and painless death occurs.

The first notification of a death goes to a statistician who arranges for the creation of a new fetus that will some day fill the work related responsibility of the just deceased. In that way the right balance of men and women is maintained and additionally the right number of workers is kept at required standards.

A question was asked about mourning the dead and friends missing the deceased. The doctor could not understand the question in as much as those concerns are more our civilization's requirements. These are not emotions that exist here. It seemed to the six of us that this is really a cold hearted civilization.

The doctor went on to state that in this city about fifty persons die each year from old age. He reiterated that by our accounts a person here lives to about three hundred years.

The sign of final days is senility and the general inability to perform required responsibilities or work. People here self diagnose and come to the hospital to be released from life in a painless procedure which the doctor calls "personal completion." To me euthanasia comes to mind.

Now some things make sense. Each year about fifty people die and that generates the need to birth fifty more individuals.

I hear what is done here and try not to be judgmental. I know if these people knew of our topside hypocrisies, emotional outbursts of violence and disrespect, they would be aghast. So how can I judge what happens here knowing people on the surface of the planet would seem pretty awful to the beings in this culture.

A final word. Death is followed by cremation. The ashes become fertilizer used in farming practices. In some ways this seems to be barbaric but I suppose some would say this is an appropriate return to nature.

August 12, 2011

Today was a most interesting and revealing day. This morning saw us gathered together (as has happened quite often before) in a small auditorium. After all six of us and our residential hosts were seated, Jonar addressed us.

"We have over the past many days asked you questions about your civilization on the surface of this planet. In addition we have many responses from you when we were learning your language. We selected a group from of our city to analyze what you have told us. From that analysis and review we have developed a few questions for you because some of what we learned about your world leaves us very perplexed."

"For example, you have words such as truth and lying. These words are opposite and yet you tell us certain people in your world will do both regularly. We understand truth to be reality and stating what is so. Yet why do you need such a word? Why would anyone say anything deliberately that they knew was incorrect?"

At this point Jonar was silent looking for an answer. I guess I punctuated the silence and stood up to respond. "There is not a good simple answer to your excellent question. We are an imperfect species. We are emotional. We are sometimes driven by greed, jealousy, pride etc. While we try to be good citizens, sometimes our nature betrays us. Even when we know right from wrong, we may do a wrong thing to advance our personal goals. There really is no complete answer, Jonar, that I could give that would satisfy you or others. Your civilization appears to be even tempered and everyone is treated fairly and similarly. You have no reason to lie and take advantage of another. Yet we do an unfair thing to another for reasons that are hard to explain. We are a long way from evolving to being like your city of inhabitants where there is only truth."

Jonar, with a quizzical look accepted my answer. He then went on to an even more revealing question. "You repeatedly tell us about God, prayer, and the word hope. We don't understand 'God'?"

At this point, surprisingly Angel Ramirez jumped in with an answer. "Our lives on the surface of the planet are uncertain. We don't know if we will live long. We don't know if we will be prosperous or poor in our lives. We care about our families, yet we don't know how happy they will be or how their futures will be determined. When we don't know important things, we need to feel that there is a supreme being with great power and wisdom who will invisibly guide our lives for good outcomes. We talk in our minds for positive results from our God and this self talk which is either mental or verbal is a prayer. The word 'hope' is our inward desire that we want the future to be good."

I thought Angel did a good job. After he was seated Jonar spoke. "We do not have a God concept and here we never have a need to lie. Our truth is our daily life. Your words and your civilization are very strange to us. We will continue to try to understand you."

"There is one last puzzling thing we have noticed. You have the word laugh and your language quite often mentions humor and jokes. Again we do not understand. We see you laugh sometimes and we do not understand why."

I guess everyone needed to take a turn at some point answering Jonar's questions. This time it was Steve Letterman.

"Jonar, we have been with your people for many days. We see you as an even emotional group. You go about your daily routines. In doing so there is obvious contentment. I guess you need nothing more. We are different. We have many different states of mind. Sometimes we are sad when things go wrong or a very bad thing happens. We may then cry or feel depressed or angry. Sometimes the opposite is true. We find ourselves in a very happy mood because of good events that touch our lives. We like to be happy and wish we could be happy all the time. The word joke is a story that induces happiness and laughter in a fellow individual. Jokes are statements that are complex, paradoxical to reality or observations that amuse us. We could tell a story of how one of your people started to wear a black suit that wasn't shiny. We might think that looked strange and we would laugh or joke about it. You would not understand why we would take amusement in such an event plus you could not conceive of anyone wearing different clothes. For that reason this analogy points up the mystery of our culture and yours. We all want to be friends but at the same time we try not to be judgmental of what we truly do not understand."

The day went on with more questions about our lives on the surface. We all took turns answering. Jonar and the others quietly listened attentively. We never really got a good insight as to whether our answers made sense to them or not.

August 28, 2011

We spent many days learning about their transportation system, the creation of a roof to this city which looks like the sky and is probably at least two thousand feet high. We learned about their lighting system, their handling of waste water and sewage and their preparation for an earth movement shift should that ever occur.

Sometimes, we mused that this long term super orientation was going beyond entertaining visitors. Amongst ourselves we did express concerns as to how long we should stay here and what long term plans might they have for us.

At the end of the day we were gathered together again. This time a new leader - Aratus, spoke to us. He had just learned English so he could communicate with our group.

"One of your questions raised by all of you in the beginning was that of knowing where we come from and how does the tunnel fit. We have a few people that are our historians. Their purpose is to conserve our archives of history. They are now going to learn English so they can answer your questions. In a few days we will take you to their building so you can be told about our origins."

September 6, 2011

What I learned about today is nothing short of astounding. It changed everything I ever thought about the evolvement of mankind. Here is how the day went.

The six of us plus our hosts were walked and shuttled to an area of the city where we had not visited before. We were taken to a rather basic two story building. After entering the building we were ushered into a reasonably large auditorium where we were seated.

Two men came from a side door and sat at a table facing us. We were seated about forty feet away. Soon after they seated themselves, they provided their names. One name given was Solink and the other was Barnia. We were told that they served as the official historians of their city civilization.

Each indicated that they hoped their English would be good enough to be understood. As far as I was concerned they came through loud and clear.

Solink started with introductions. It was Barnia who was slated to give our presentation. It went something like this.

Many hundreds of thousands of years in the past is when their history starts. What they know is that around the globe there were hundreds of pockets of nomadic very primitive peoples. These people for the most part lived in caves and survived by hunting animals and sometimes finding edible plants. They believed they communicated with grunts and hand signals primarily. Their groups could range in size from a few dozen to occasionally several hundred people.

These very barbaric creatures had features which were different from you or us. Their only advance at the time were some stone tools and hunting implements. They knew about fire. That was it. The timeline might be anywhere from eight hundred thousand years ago to perhaps two million years. We are derived from these barbaric people but not in a way you would expect.

There was a time that visitors from elsewhere landed on this planet. We don't know who they were or where they came from. We do know they discovered these nomadic groups of people. They did something extraordinary. From around the globe they visited these barbarians and began testing their babies for a certain level of native intelligence. Occasionally they would find a child with far above intellectual activity. When they did, they left an offering for the parents and took the child with them.

Over a period of one year approximately fifty children were extracted from their homes and taken to a small preserve in an area you now call New Mexico on your maps. The temperatures were mild and the visiting beings and the gathered children set up a learning center.

These advanced beings began to school these children in language, rudimentary science, and skills which would be necessary to survive. This village of human adoption and learning existed for almost two hundred years. When the visiting beings left, the remaining humans numbered several thousand people as they were then into their ninth generation.

From that nucleus of educational and scientific cauldron, we were created. We were homogeneous. We never ventured far from our New Mexico area home and most certainly did not attempt to contact any of the barbaric indigenous people who lived anywhere else on the planet.

Over the next one hundred thousand years we thrived as a civilization. We became scientifically advanced, probably far beyond the technology all of you currently enjoy now on the surface of your planet. We were a race in pursuit of advancement. If we had ever experienced your emotions of desire, greed, ego, anger, despair, jealousy etc, we genetically engineered our offspring so that we eliminated those characteristics of people which we deemed harmful. We were up to almost two million persons by the time some particular events took place. We had developed four cities that we believe were very advanced beyond what we have been told your current cities are like. We prospered and were able to achieve considerable longevity. Diseases had been wiped out for thousands of years.

Our scientists discovered through the study of climates that an event was about to occur which would be devastating to our environment. We calculated that in about ten thousand years in the future, there would be a profound period of cooling that would last for several hundred thousand years or perhaps longer. Our studies showed that eventually a glacial ice build-up would bury our cities and render them useless. Everything we knew would be destroyed with the coming glacial movement.

We did not know the global extent of this expected all-consuming glacial environment, but we planned on the worst. With the assumption of total devastation to the planet's surface, we faced two options.

Although we advanced air travel and understood the universe from a telescope perspective, we were unsure if travel to another planet would be successful. This presented a quandary to us. The vast majority of persons in our advanced civilization wanted to venture away from our planet in hopes of finding a hospitable planet elsewhere. We had the technology and time to develop the passenger spacecraft which would be required. We knew life existed elsewhere because our own history showed how we were somewhat incubated by beings that came from somewhere in the universe.

About five percent of our people were very afraid of this adventure into the unknown. The theory we held was that an interim underground civilization could be created until a future period witnessed a glacial withdrawal that would allow us to return to the planet's surface.

While several thousand years passed, we gradually evacuated the planet. At the same time we created the tunnel and underground cities you see today. The project that created the tunnel and our three cities took almost two thousand years to build.

When we finally left the surface, we had a prepared city that allowed us to flourish. We reduced our population over time to the size population we now have which we considered optimal.

What really changed was that after living here for hundreds of thousands of years, we never had any desire to return to the surface of this world. We have pictures of our surface cities that were probably destroyed by the coming glaciers. At that point Solink pressed a button on a hand-held object and the screen on the large wall in front of us lit up. We were shown dozens of photographs in succession. The pictures depicted beautiful cities. The buildings were tall and shined in the glistening sunlight. Aerial flight traffic was evident everywhere. There was an absence of abundant foliage, but some trees were none-the-less visible from these pictures.

There were a few pictures of the ancestors of these current day peoples. We noticed the somewhat similar features of the people now with the exception of the skull not being quite as elongated.

Pictures were taken of spacecraft which were being readied to evacuate most of the population. It was hard to judge size from pictures but I would guess these spacecraft were at least two hundred yards in length and a wingspan of about one half that distance. There were not any close-up pictures of these craft.

The conclusion of this lecture was handled by Solink. The building we were in served as a library of sorts as well as an archive of all records. Every citizen of this city is at some point exposed to their history.

It was interesting to note the lack of inquisitiveness of these people. Although their surface civilization was advanced, they appeared to have no interest in space exploration. To me this is peculiar since their own origin makes it clear that extra terrestrial intelligence exists. It was only being faced with extinction from a glacial onslaught that prompted these people to reach out for discovering the universe.

The people of this city seem to have little interest or care about those people who fled into the universe in spacecraft seeking a new home. There is an attitude of general complacency here that is so different from our current human race.

After the meeting was over, I sauntered over to Barnia and asked him whether there has ever been any interest in going to the surface to see what life is like. I received a very curious reply. In a matter of fact manner I was told that this question could not be answered at this time. Barnia said he would take my question up with others.

For a civilization that prides itself on truthfulness and open-ness, this was a very shocking reply.

September 10, 2011

Today Joe and I were separated out from our group when we started our morning tour. The other four were taken to learn about the system of air purification which exists here. Joe and I were escorted by Denar and Rekak to an elevator. This elevator went very deep under the city and we surmised we were at the deepest point yet visited.

We entered a door which led to a room which was enormous. An object of immense size was sitting in the center of the cavernous area. This object was covered by a huge drape which concealed the nature of this object.

We stood there, somewhat dumfounded by the enormity of this very strange room. After a few minutes a female came over and introduced herself to us as Lendot. It was clear she was in charge of this area as she communicated to several other men and women who took up positions around the huge draped object.

Lendot quickly got to the reason for our visit. "Several days ago you were educated as to the origin of our underground civilization. At the end of that lecture, you addressed Barnia and asked if we were ever interested in going to the surface of the planet to see what life was like. The answer was yes but Barnia was not authorized to talk to you about that subject. He posed your question to others"

"It has been decided by us that both you and Joe are above the others in intellectual understanding. What we will now share with you shall not be told to your companions. In anticipation of today, I was asked to learn your language so that your question could be answered."

"Sixty-four years ago we launched two travel craft to go through the tunnel and visit the surface. These two craft were very advanced and it took almost five years to complete their construction. Each craft was manned by a crew of four. This building is almost directly below the tunnel floor entrance."

"These two craft were sent out with one following the other at an interval of ten minutes. The trip through the tunnel was scheduled to take approximately two hours."

"Our experience was disastrous. The second craft to emerge from the topside tunnel entrance immediately received a distress call from the travel craft that proceeded it. What they learned was that the first ship to fly out experienced a bombardment of radio signals in the air that interfered with the ship's navigational function. The crew could not properly fly and control any flight path. By the time the second ship emerged, the distress was so acute that it was apparent that all controls in the first craft were no longer functioning and a crash was evident. The last communication from the first craft before it crashed was to warn the second craft to immediately return to the tunnel and seal the door behind them. Before the door was closed by the second returning craft, explosive charges were set around the area in front of the tunnel door. They were set in such a manner that exploding rocks and dust would be directed to conceal the tunnel entrance. Those charges were initiated on a remote signal basis from inside the tunnel once the door was shut.

We know the first ship traveled at considerable speed once it emerged from the tunnel after having forced the door open and blasted through any rock or earth obstructions. The crew of the second ship calculated the speed and trajectory of the first craft. When we mind probed your group of six several months ago we deciphered a map of the area where the entrance to the door was situated geographically. We believe the first ship would have crashed in the vicinity of the town you call Roswell, New Mexico.

"We will now uncover the second ship which has been at rest here for the past sixty-four years."

At this point Lendot gave a hand signal and the huge drape was lifted off the sitting space craft. I have never seen anything like it.

We were informed it measured thirty eight feet in width with a length of almost one hundred feet. It was like a work of art.

It was shiny black. There were no windows or viewing ports visible. It did not rest on wheels, but sat directly on the ground. We were told it could lift vertically when activated. There was no doorway at all visible.

Joe asked how a ship that wide could travel at what he calculated as fourteen hundred miles per hour through the narrow tunnel and not smash into the side walls of the tunnel. It was explained that the entire tunnel has sensors built into the walls. Those sensors operated in unison with the sensors in the space craft so a smooth even trajectory was maintained.

We asked if it was possible to see the inside of this sleek and awing craft. As we walked over to the front half of the spaceship, one of the attendant workers wheeled over a stair ladder. Even where the ladder met the skin of the ship there was no evidence of an opening.

Lendot came over and pressed a hand held device that rang out with a high pitched code. The code was unrecognizable to me, but Joe knew right away how we could duplicate the sound. After this code was sounded, a doorway appeared as a thin section of the craft's skin slid into an opening much like a sliding pocket door in a house.

We followed Lendot up the stairs into the craft. The craft obviously sensed our movements and lighting was instantly available.

Joe and I were amazed. It was like the reality of all science fiction movies we had ever seen all put together. Most of the craft (the rear two thirds) were dedicated to the propulsion system.

The front of the craft had a huge bridge whose four seats were set up directly facing a multitude of controls and lights. Several screens were evident. At the touch of a switch by Lendot, the screens activated and we saw the huge hanger area in front of the aircraft. One screen also showed visibility to the left, right, and rear.

We left the ship which closed its doors behind us after our departure. The crew of the second ship was still alive and they had been summoned to meet with us today. Three men and one woman came forward after being called over by Lendot. Lendot served as an interpreter since none of these former pilots/ crew were yet taught our language.

Joe and I literally bombarded them with a battery of questions which must have lasted at least two hours. All of our litany of questions was patiently answered. A summary of what we learned is as follows:

First of all there is no emotion of fear or dread so this crew went forth on this journey in an intrepid manner. Clearly they were disturbed by the crash of the first ship but there was no emotion of remorse. The second ship saw only about ten seconds of the earth's surface before they turned around to head back in after the warning from the other craft before it crashed.

Joe and I learned there is no interest in again venturing out. We couldn't believe they would just give up after this one terrible set-back. Joe even said he could help them insulate the ship from radio wave interference so that a second venture would be successful. Our enthusiasm for trying again was definitely not shared.

The meeting concluded with Lendot once again asking us to keep what we learned to ourselves. Before leaving, Joe again asked to hear the sounds that opened the spacecraft. His request was obliged and Joe was convinced he could easily duplicate the sound if he had to do so. I was frankly perplexed by his interest and thought he was going to hatch some kind of escape plan someday. Later in the day Joe told me his real reason for learning the coded sound and I must say I was more than astounded by what he told me.

September 13, 2011

Today we were all taken to an auditorium where we were told we would spend several weeks trying to be instructed in the language of these people. At first we dug in to the task not giving the activity any real thought.

Later it occurred to us that the only reason this instruction would be planned was that there was an intent to have us become permanent residents. This was a chilling thought. We up to now thought of ourselves as guests. Now we were beginning to feel like we might be captives.

Joe is bolder than I, so he asked Jonar who was at our language session, when they planned to let us leave and return back to the surface. The directness of the question caught me off guard. Our companions became instantly silent when Joe posed the question.

Jonar looked Joe straight in the eye and responded. I will never forget his words. "How can we allow you to return to your dysfunctional civilization with the knowledge that you have about us. We have always welcomed you here with our intent of making you one of us. You can never leave. Please do not ask this again"

All six of us stood there stupefied and frozen in place. Angel tried to jest with "I guess

I won't get my three hundred thousand dollar payout now." Normally we would have found this amusing. We all felt sick inside.

September 15, 2011

Once again Joe took the lead on the issue of captivity. At the end of today's language lesson Joe went over to Jonar.

"Jonar I know you said it was final that we stay here and not return. I think you should reconsider. I have some compelling information to talk to you about that you have not considered. Your failure to hear me explain why we should return, will cause your civilization to be far more at risk than if we left."

I actually saw an almost worried look on Jonar's face. He quickly regained his composure. "I will arrange a forum for you to make a last appeal with your reasons. I will set this up soon." Jonar walked off and our instructional day ended on this very tense note.

September 17, 2011

All six of us were taken to a room where a long table was set up. We six sat on one side and five individuals sat opposite us. Jonar was one of the five. Jonar was to be the interpreter.

Jonar started off our meeting. He was very direct. "What are these compelling reasons why we should allow all of you to return?"

Joe calmly, yet forcefully responded. "You must know our visit was not a secret. Others on the surface manufactured our tunnel vehicles. Also others provided food for our journey. Right now people are standing guard at the tunnel entrance. It took many more people to be involved in finally opening the tunnel door and extinguishing the protective vacuum which existed."

"We have been gone for months. There is a plan established that will send another reserve crew down here if they do not hear from us in six months. If you capture them, another reserve crew will be sent. Even if you destroy the tunnel, consider this. Our civilization will be made aware of your existence underground. We may not know who or what you are but we will know you are here."

"We are billions of beings on the

surface. Our technology gets better every year. Knowing you are here, you become priority one to get here and discover your world. Our curiosity will never let us relent. It may take a thousand years, but we will eventually drill our own tunnels to reach you."

"In short, you may buy some time by keeping us captive and eventually capturing rescue crews, but rest assured, your secret existence is known and we will never quit.

I have never witnessed as profound a silence as what occurred when Jonar translated what Joe had said. Jonar held a very long conversation with the other four at the table. Not understanding what they were saying, we just sat there and listened and watched for any expression.

Joe is probably the brightest of us and I think he picked up on some of their language during the past few days of instruction.

We actually witnessed the beginning of an argument between members of the panel. The back and forth discussion went on for almost two hours. During that time Joe picked up a few phrases that he could interpret. Some of those deciphered partial sentences went as follows: "never trusted, eventual destruction, prisoners, can be friends, their culture, how can we control, when ultimate decision." At the end of the two hours, Jonar came over to us and said "it was undecided what to do. The matter will be turned over to additional individuals to gather further input. We may have an answer in a very few days. In the meantime please be cooperative and continue the language lessons."

We walked away from the meeting with some hope. We vowed that even if we got "no" for an answer, we would never stop trying to reason with these people and plea for our return to the surface.

As I go to bed tonight, I find it interesting to see how dispassionate Denar and Rekak are toward the whole affair. They show no signs of anger or sympathy. I know they comprehend the turmoil we are trying to deal with but they provide no response at all.

September 21, 2011

Joe and I were summoned to meet with the panel that was considering our fate. Interestingly just the two of us were there to hear the verdict. The other four members of our team were probably taken to the language lesson.

We sat down along with Denar and Rekak. It was a tense two minutes of silence before Jonar stood up from the seated panel of judges or deciders. He was not brief and I hope my log tonight captures the jist of what was spoken.

"We speak to Ike and Joe. What we shall tell you can not be spoken to your other four explorer friends. This was a very difficult decision for us to make. We have decided to let some of you return. There are many conditions. First of all both of you must stay. You may be allowed to leave in a few years if you so choose, but not now."

"The others may go. We are going to have to adjust their memories so that there is no knowledge of us and the experiences they have shared since arrival. We have the ability to do this without any harm to them. From the point that the end of the tunnel was found until they are released back to your journey craft, they will have no memory. Further we will adjust their memories so that they will report that the two of you died."

"Ike we know that you keep a log of your daily activities here with your computer. You may or may not have realized that your entries were monitored by us. We take no offense at anything you have written. Further we are going to have you write some additional notes. We will see that your log disks are provided to take to the surface to be read by whoever has officiated this exploration. There are some special requests you need to make so that we feel comfortable letting your four friends return."

"You shall request that the topside tunnel door which is now open, be shut. We shall once again create a vacuum chamber. The tunnel opening must once again be disguised. We do not want anyone to visit us again. We ask that you plead with your associates on the surface to keep this entire exploration secret."

"There is a personal matter that is very important to us that we will request you journal into your log. We will give you these instructions just before the release of your friends."

"As for the two of you. We have felt from the beginning that both of you, unlike the others, have a greater capacity to understand us and learn what we have to offer. We welcome your continuing to stay among us. You will need to learn our language. We will teach you a great deal and you will become a part of us. Your knowledge of the surface civilization will be important to understand. We now know there will be a time when your civilization will be allowed to know of us and that we can all respect each other's culture and live in harmony. However, your civilization has a lot to learn about respect for other living beings."

"In five or ten years we will allow you to leave with your memories intact if you so choose. By that time you will be more a part of us and we believe we will be more trusting of your protecting our existence. As an inducement to staying, you probably would live about two hundred years longer here if you stayed as opposed to a shorter life span on the surface. We are certain you will give this a good deal of thought."

After Jonar finished, he asked if we clearly understood what he had said and wondered if we had any questions. Joe asked a couple of quick questions which were politely answered.

We were dismissed along with Denar and Rekak. We joined the rest of our group in the language lab. Steve and Niles asked where we were. We gave a lie about their asking us if we had further reasons why we should be allowed to leave. I said Joe and I had a few more. I said they still had not made a decision.

September 28, 2011

After our language session, but before supper, Jonar came to our residence unit and gave me the log entries to put into my computer disk.

Jonar said that we should have one more day with our four friends. We would all still go to the language unit tomorrow as if there was nothing different. At the end of the day our four friends will be put into a more unconscious state once they fall asleep. Memory adjustment work will take place during the rest of the evening. They will awake on the other side of the tunnel door with no recollection as to the passage of time or our existence. They will journey out without missing you and will only later vaguely remember that you both had somehow died.

It took almost two hours for me to add the final log entries and special request by Jonar, which you will read on Disk #3 after my last Sept. 28th entry. Please fulfill all the conditions set forth. We promised that you would.

Joe and I are okay. Knowing we can leave in five or ten years is enough to sustain us. Right now I think we will come back. Keep the yellow ribbon on my office door.

Love - Ike

Chapter 36
November 19, 2011

As Mike arrived at his office door at 8:00 a.m., he saw John seated outside already waiting for him. Mike said, "Hi, good morning, I am really not surprised to see you here waiting. Come on in, we have a lot to discuss." Before the door closed, Mike asked his secretary that they not be disturbed for any reason.

John sat down in the chair across from Mike's desk. "I have to say Mike, I was never more captivated by what I was reading than I was last night. I frankly got very little sleep after a second reading. I never dreamed where this tunnel project was going to go. I am still disbelieving what I know to be true."

Mike sat back in his chair. "John, I read it twice also. God, I'm going to miss Ike. It will be hard counting out five or ten years until he surfaces, if of course he does. Almost everlasting life is difficult to run away from."

"Mike I think we can easily handle the explanations for Ike and Joe's temporary disappearance. There is very little family for each of them. We shall keep both men on our payroll, do tax returns and keep the myth of their existence going. That's the easy part. Harder will be to keep everyone quiet who has been a part of this project."

"Somehow," Mike replied "we can close off the tunnel and create a myth about it going nowhere. If we don't make it a big deal and keep the people involved separated, I think it will go away. As time goes by memories fade. Speaking of memories, now we know why our four explorers came back not remembering anything. Can you imagine a society with such sophistication that surgical memory expulsion is an easy chore?"

"John, you and I are the only two people in this world who know about something that happened hundreds of thousands of years ago and spawned a lost civilization that was way technically advanced beyond where we are today. Remember when Ike said he was told that our tunnel took two thousand years to create. My God what a feat!"

"Mike, we have a lot to do to close up the tunnel and satisfy that part of Ike's bargain. I will get that started. I think we can have the tunnel door sealed and the entrance covered up in two weeks. When that door closes, Jonar will know that we are doing our best to live up to Ike's promise."

"Look John, while you do that, I am going to think of a way to fulfill Jonar's very special requests on the third disk. This is going to be very tricky. I'll let you know when I have a plan."

Chapter 37
December 2, 2011

Mike and John met in the executive conference room at 10:30 a.m. John spread out ten photographs on the conference room table. "Mike, five of these are aerial shots and the rest are ground shots at fifty feet out to two hundred yards. What do you think?"

"I think" Mike responded. "That there is absolutely no sign of our tunnel. Nice concealment job."

"Yeah Mike," John replied. "I think so too. I used a team who already knew about the project. They were told we hit a dead end and were under a government order by an environmental office to put things back the way it used to be. I don't think these people on the team will think much about this as the months and years go by."

"I agree John" Mike answered "I'll bet right now Jonar and company are sucking air out of that chamber as we speak!"

John cut in. "So how are you doing on that amazing request of Jonar?"

Mike sat back. "I'm still not sure we have a plan yet. Because of the secrecy involved we have to do this mostly ourselves. Here are a few pencil notes that are possible ideas. What do you think?" At that point Mike handed John three separate sheets of lined paper with each one having six to twelve steps in an action plan."

"Mike" John stated after a few minutes to study

the handouts, "I'm not sure any of these totally works. I see problems with each of them. Your sheet marked plan number two seems close. Maybe I can take it with me, tweak it, and get back to you."

"John, be my guest" Mike was quick to offer. "No idea is a bad idea. This is going to one tricky deal and it can't come back to our doorstep by any means."

"Mike" John said "You know I think about Ike and Joe every day. I'm haunted by the fact they are living a subterranean life and we may never see them again."

"Look John" Mike said with note of sorrow in his voice "I feel as you do. I miss Ike a lot. I guess I keep going with the thought they will return. Every day I hope and pray for them."

Chapter 38
December 4, 2011

Today Ike and Joe were brought to a conference room in a small auditorium. It was a welcome break from the intensity of the language laboratory.

Jonar made a hand signal for both Ike and Joe to be seated. "I have something important to talk to you about. Five days ago the tunnel door on the surface was closed. We are almost done making the tunnel chamber a vacuum. So far your friends on the surface are following the request from your log. We are very relieved."

"Jonar" Ike said "I know my business partners. They can be trusted to do everything they were asked to accomplish including that very unusual special request that you had me put into the third disk."

"Ike and Joe" Jonar uttered with an almost trace of a smile. "Speaking for myself, Denar, Rekak and others, we are glad to have you here!"

Joe replied quickly "YYK ACK NIK DOK VILP SIG NAY YOK KICK JAY LIDE SU JANSO"

Jonar actually smiled and walked off after saying "LITA ZAY KIG"

Ike looked at Joe. "You really amazed me. I got some of that but not all."

"Well Ike, you might have learned more if you stayed in the lab each day. I noticed you have been taking two hour breaks twice a week." Joe finished with a tone of expecting an answer.

"Joe, I find their little house of sexual release somewhat compelling from time to time. I consider this also part of my assimilation program.

Joe looked at Ike and started to laugh out loud.

Chapter 39
March 12, 2012

At the request of Mike Dennis, John Nelson arrived at Mike's office at 3:00 p.m. on Monday, March 12, 2012. He sat down on the chair across from Mike's desk. He already knew what was going to be discussed.

Mike started out. "Well, John, what do you think of the plan."

John leaned forward with several pages of paper in his hand. He shuffled the pages for a minute and replied, "I supposed it's the one marked plan five that you are going to use?"

"Right on" Mike smiled as he answered. "I thought it provided the best chance of success with the least risk. I have a helicopter pilot that I trust and I will be going along to make sure this works. We have watched the perimeter of the military installation for two weeks from a hillside about three miles away. I have four other persons I trust using very high resolution day and night vision optics. We know when any guards make their rounds. On Thursday morning about 3:15 a.m. is when we will go in with guided communication from our spotter.

"Mike, it sounds easy on paper, but I can think of a lot that can backfire and you would have a lot of explaining to do if it did. Have you thought about what you would do if you were found out. The whole company is vulnerable if this goes wrong." John had a very apprehensive expression on his face.

"John," Mike said "Don't think I have not thought about the problems we could create if this blows up in our faces. Sometimes you just have to venture forward into the unknown and hope for the best. We owe it to Ike to fulfill his promise to Jonar."

Mike continued. "Over on the table is the package. I have been very careful to make sure none of the paper, packaging, or anything else is traceable. No fingerprints are evident."

"Okay Mike, I'm with you." John sat back with still a level of tension showing on his face. "Mike, if you decide last minute not to do this, I would certainly understand. Jonar would never know one way or another. In fact only Ike would know if he returned and frankly he could deal with this in five years or so. There really is no rush here."

"John, as of now we do this on Thursday morning. I will keep you advised as to how it went. Wish me luck."

Both men stood up and shook hands before John walked out of Mike's office.

At the end of the day, Mike felt compelled to go to Ike's office. Once inside, he starred for a few minutes at the empty desk before him. He said a silent prayer, walked out, closing the door behind him.

The end.

Epilogue
March 15, 2012 8:16 a.m.
Groom Lake Air Force Base, Nevada

Sergeant Cooper knocked twice on the closed door which would enter the duty officer's lounge station at Groom Lake Airbase in Nevada. The duty office responded with a quick "come in."

After opening the door, Sergeant Cooper stood straight at attention in front of the duty officer's desk. A quick salute was given and returned. "Major, we had an event this morning."

Major Hiddle was a short, partially balding man with broad shoulders and muscular girth. He looked up at the Sergeant with the expectant countenance of (oh boy here we go). "Yes, Sergeant, what happened?"

After being called to at ease, Sergeant Cooper began with a crisp dialogue. "Sir, at o' four-thirty hours, our sentries at the southwest perimeter thought they heard the rotors of a helicopter. It was too far away to tell for sure, and they reported that the sounds only lasted for about twenty seconds and then ended."

"If it was a helicopter, Major, it had to be coming in at a very low altitude because nothing was picked up on our radar."

"Sir, at o' six hundred, a roving sentry unit found a large package on our side of the electrified fence. It's location would be pretty close to where the brief helicopter sounds were heard. It is presumed because the wrapped package weighs about twelve pounds, that it had to have been dropped on our side of the fence by the helicopter. Since our fence is sixteen feet high, I don't think anyone could easily toss a twelve pound package over the fence."

"We were suspicious of course when we found the package. We had dogs sniff for explosives, and used a portable x-ray to determine the contents. It appears to be all cardboard outside, interior wrapping and bubble wrap and paper contents. No metal, plastic or anything other than paper."

"Sir the package is addressed in large letters saying FOR THE BASE COMMANDING OFFICER ONLY"

Major Hiddle sat back in his swivel chair with his arm laying relaxed across his chest. "Well, Sergeant Cooper, where in this package now?"

Sergeant Cooper quickly replied. "Sir it is in the other room. I can bring it in."

Major Hiddle smiled. "Forthwith Sergeant, let's see what we've got here."

Sergeant Cooper did a quick about face and went out of the room. He was back in about twenty seconds cradling a large two foot by two foot brown cardboard package with a thin rope weaving around the package. When placed on Major Hiddle's duty officer's desk, you could plainly see the two inch bold letters addressing the package to the commanding officer.

Major Hiddle picked up the package and gently shook it. "Yeah, it seems like just cardboard and paper. Someone went to a lot of expense and effort to get this to us. The question is do I open it or take it to Colonel

Orbach."

After a few seconds of thought, Major Hiddle picked up the duty phone and called Colonel Orbach's residence. After the phone was answered by a woman, Major Hiddle announced himself and asked if Colonel Orbach could please take the call. About a minute later the phone was answered. "Orbach here!!"

"Good morning Colonel, this is the duty officer Major Hiddle. Sir, I would like to brief you on an event that occurred this morning." A quick three minute recap of what happened was synopsized for Colonel Orbach.

"Well Tom this certainly is strange." Colonel Orbach started out. "Since it's just papers, have it delivered to my office to open. I'll be in at o' nine-thirty."

"Yes sir," Major Hiddle responded, "I'll have the package placed on your desk." There was a brief good-bye.

Chapter 40
March 15, 2012
9:48 a.m.
Groom Lake Air Force Base, Nevada

Before Colonel Orbach opened the package, he called in Lieutenant Tiels to serve as a witness, "Well, here goes." Colonel Orbach proceeded to cut the thin twine and used a box knife to split the taped seams of the package. As the cardboard exterior fell away, there were several inches of bubble wrap. Once the bubble wrap was removed, a large manila envelope was pulled free. It was likewise addressed to be only opened by the Commanding Officer of the Air Force Base at Groom Lake, Nevada. There were no markings as to who sent the package.

Colonel Orbach opened the envelope quickly. He took the four double spaced typed pages to his desk where he sat down to read the contents aloud so Lieutenant Tiels could witness what message was delivered. It took ten minutes to read the four pages. At the completion of reading the contents, Colonel Orbach quickly picked up the phone to his secretary. "Ann put through an emergency high priority call to Lieutenant General Nicholas Dermit at the Pentagon. Put the call through to me immediately when he picks up."

Colonel Orbach looked up at Lieutenant Tiels

who had an astonished look on his face. "Lieutenant, what you heard today is highly classified and is not too be discussed with anyone, is that clear?"

"Yes sir Colonel," Lieutenant Tiels turned around and left the colonel's office after receiving a formal dismissal.

March 15, 2012
1:30 p.m.
Washington DC - The Pentagon

General Dermit paced in his spacious office until two more Air Force generals came in. Gentleman, a situation has developed at our Groom Lake Air Base in Nevada. I'm going to fly there tomorrow. Here is a list of three scientists who you will convince to drop what they are doing. They are to catch the first planes they can to get to Groom Lake tomorrow. They will be reimbursed for any flight costs and expenses. A generous consulting fee will be paid by the Air Force. If a commercial plane is not available, get one of our military planes to them. This is really important."

General Dermit dismissed the other two generals and picked up the phone. His call went right to Colonel Orbach at Groom Lake. On pick up he spoke. "Andy, I am coming out there tomorrow with three scientists. Make everything ready for us to get going. Also, get a flute player and record those notes in as many ways as possible. I want that recording ready when we arrive. Also, get housing for the four of us since we may need to stay there for a day or two.

March 16, 2012
11:25 a.m.
Groom Lake Air Force Base, Nevada

Colonel Orbach was at the tarmac as General Dermit's Air Force jet landed. He was greeted personally and driven across the base to a large brown metal hanger. The four guards quickly saluted and passed the Colonel's jeep inside.

"General there it is over there." Colonel Orbach pointed to a far corner of the hanger.

"Colonel, I always wondered about this as to whether this was true or not. This has been under wraps for over sixty years and frankly I never gave the stories much credence."

"Colonel" General Dermit continued. "Have any of the scientists arrived?"

"Yes Sir, all three are here and waiting over there for your arrival." Colonel Orbach answered.

General Dermit walked over to the scientists and thanked them for coming. Each of them was an esteemed expert in various technological disciplines and they had served many times as special consultants to the U.S. Air Force.

General Dermit addressed the group after receiving the typed four page message handed to him by Colonel Orbach. "Gentlemen, you know what your have in front of you. Now I will read something that will bring this whole matter to life so to speak."

"This letter is addressed to only be opened by the Commanding Officer of the Groom Lake Air Force Base in Nevada otherwise know as Area 51."

On June 22, 1947 a spacecraft crashed landed near Roswell, New Mexico. The spacecraft was obviously quickly commandeered and brought to a holding place at Groom Lake Air Force Base where it has been in storage for almost sixty-five years.

We have no doubt that you have tried to enter the spacecraft using any means available. You have not been unsuccessful because the black composite skin is impenetrable.

This letter is a gift to the Air Force and to the United States. We are providing you with a method to enter the spacecraft.

When you enter, you will have available the possibility of learning about a technology that for exceeds anything that is currently available. This spacecraft has no weaponry. However, the advanced designs of technologies employed will greatly advance United States military and commercial interests. Your technological gain will not be a quick event. It will take you many years to understand what you see before you. It will take much longer to begin to harness the capabilities which are being presented to you.

This gift comes at a request to do a service. This spacecraft had four crew which obviously died on impact or shortly thereafter. You will likely find them in a now decomposed state wearing shiny metallic cloth jumpsuits. It is requested that the four bodies be cremated and the ashes dispersed. Please do not do scientific studies on the corpses. This would be very offensive to the race that created the spacecraft and sent it on its failed mission. We tell you now that these four beings are very human-like despite the fact that they are all about six foot four inches tall with a very elongated skull structure. Please respect their lives and quickly cremate the body remains.

To enter the spacecraft, use a flute and do consecutive three second notes as follows with the highest pitch possible. Play notes A and F. At the front of the spacecraft, twelve feet back from the nose, a door will slide open if the notes have played correctly.

When you enter the spacecraft, the air will be pure and clean. There is an air purification system that is far beyond any you are familiar with currently. It would still be operable. In fact all the operations of the ship are for the most part functional unless damaged by impact. The power source is so advanced that the systems of this craft could operate for at least five hundred years before needing some maintenance attention.

Please use this gift wisely. It is granted to you on the faith that the human race on the planet will try to become more compassionate, civilized, and responsible. Future gifts are possible if wise choices are made.

Do not attempt to determine the origin of this message. Do not attempt to track down the helicopter that delivered the message. This is an act of good faith and generosity and should not be scrutinized or investigated.

Signed - Guardians of the Planet

"Well Gentlemen" General Dermit continued. "Let's try the flute recordings."

The third flute sequence played caused the aircraft door to quietly slide back into its housing pocket. The interior of the ship was fully lighted and welcoming.

General Dermit was first to enter the spacecraft looking back at the others and stating, "Looks like the Area 51 mystery is finally solved!"

ORDER FORM

The book "Tunnel Vision" can be ordered at $9.50 per copy. This price is inclusive of shipping and handling plus any legally required sales taxes.

<u>ORDER QTY</u>   <u>COST</u>   <u>EXTENDED COST</u>

_____   <u>$9.50</u>   _____

Please make a check payable to the author "Ronald Phillips." Send your order to:

> Ronald Phillips
> 109 Limekiln Drive
> Neenah, Wisconsin 54956